Eleanor Hill

Eleanor Hill

Lisa Williams Kline

Front Street / Cricket Books
Chicago

—For Mommis

Library of Congress Cataloging-in-Publication Data

Kline, Lisa Williams.

Eleanor Hill/Lisa Williams Kline.—1st ed.

p.   cm.

Summary: In the early years of the twentieth century, inspired by a free-thinking

teacher and determined not to get married and stay trapped in her

North Carolina fishing village, teenage Eleanor sets

out to seek her chosen path of living as an independent woman.

ISBN 0-8126-2715-6

[1. Sex role Fiction.   2. Family life—North Carolina Fiction.

3. North Carolina Fiction.] I. Title.

PZ7.K67935El   1999

[Fic]—dc21   99-16090

Contents

PART ONE

Atlantic Grove

Sand Crabs
and Suffragettes

Eleanor had been helping Papa mend his fishnet and was late for school, but she stole one minute to climb the pile of oyster shells next to the fish shack. The pile was as tall as a house, bleached white except for the new purple-hued shells on top, and it glinted in the sun like a magic mountain. The fishermen were checking the sails on their sharpies, and the women were busy with chores, so there was no one looking, no one to shout, "Eleanor Hill, get down from there! Climbing is not ladylike!" She scrambled to the summit, the shells crunching under her lace-up school shoes.

From the top of the pile she could see the sails of Papa's sharpie, named *Annis H* after her mother, as he headed out to fish. Across the sound was the Outer Banks, a thin sliver of green on a pink horizon, lit from behind with a steady brightness where the sun was getting ready to rise. To the north was the Neuse River, and a two-hour ride on the mailboat got you to New Bern, one of the biggest cities in North Carolina.

The fall wind off the sound was cold, and Eleanor

pulled her sweater tight around her. Suddenly the red edge of the sun popped into view. School! She clambered down the oyster pile, pounded down the dirt path past Mr. Fulcher's store, past the whitewashed Church of Two Hundred Trees, and slid behind her wooden desk at Atlantic Grove Academy.

Miss Rosalie, her back to the class, was writing the date, "Tuesday, November 12, 1912," and listing classwork on the board. She wore her shiny dark hair swept up in an elegant bun that Eleanor tried to imitate at home. Virgie Mae, Eleanor's best friend, shot her a questioning look with one eyebrow raised.

"Mending Papa's fishing net," Eleanor mouthed, acting out a sewing motion. Virgie Mae made a sympathetic face.

Still catching her breath, Eleanor opened her desk to get out her tablet. She noticed Nat Taylor watching her with a funny, crooked grin. Just as she put her hand inside the desk, she heard a furious scratching, and something pinched her hard.

"Owww!" She yanked her hand out of the desk. A six-inch sand crab gripped her index finger. There were shrieks and laughter from the children around her.

Eleanor had been bitten by crabs plenty of times. She gave her hand a powerful shake and the crab flew across the room, slid over Adeline Fulcher's desk, and fell on the floor. Adeline, who was only seven and small for her age, screamed and pulled her feet up on the seat of her chair. Sam Bynum ran toward the crab, brandishing his ruler like a sword.

Miss Rosalie's skirt whirled as she turned to face the

children. "Each of you in your seat this instant!" Chair legs scraped as all fifteen of them obeyed.

Meanwhile the crab had backed itself under the teacher's desk, standing high on its spindly legs and waving its sand-colored claws. Its antennae circled wildly.

Eleanor examined her finger. A bright drop of blood seeped from the puncture and grew bigger and bigger, like a red balloon. She stuck her finger in her mouth. It barely hurt at all, really.

Miss Rosalie cautiously bent down, reached one slim hand toward the crab, and then withdrew it. The children laughed and cried, "Miss Rosalie's a scaredy-cat!"

"I'll get the broom!" Eleanor said, running to the closet. She wished the class wouldn't laugh at Miss Rosalie. She loved everything about their new teacher, from the way she said all her *ings* to how she cocked her head when she listened to something Eleanor said. When the students went out in the schoolyard for recess, Miss Rosalie sat at her desk with her back very straight and read thick textbooks, writing careful notes. Once Eleanor saw her mending her socks, and another time, when she glanced up from hopscotch, her teacher had her head on her desk.

Miss Rosalie looked grateful when Eleanor handed her the broom, and she tried to sweep the crab outside. Instead it grabbed the broomstraws and hung on for dear life. The class howled. After two rides on the end of the broom, the crab went sailing out into the sandy schoolyard. None of the students dared leave their seats again, but they craned their necks to see out the window.

Adeline Fulcher squeaked, "It's dead!"

But the crab was not dead, because it skittered sideways to the edge of a clump of sea grass and began to dig in a sort of frenzy, tossing clumps of sand behind it. Soon it had dug a small hole in the sand and disappeared.

"Who is responsible for this?" Miss Rosalie's voice was flat and angry.

Eleanor glanced at Nat Taylor, who was studying the floor, his black hair flopping in his eyes. If he didn't admit it, she wasn't going to tattle on him. She removed her finger from her mouth and examined it. The bleeding had stopped.

Miss Rosalie stood at the front of the classroom, tapping her ruler on her palm with a slow, measured rhythm. "If someone doesn't step forward, there will be no recess. For anyone."

The class remained silent, but Virgie Mae, Adeline, and Ben Willis all stared at Nat. He was thirteen, and no one expected him to come back to school after this year. He would help his father fish on his two-masted sharpie, like the other older boys.

"Mr. Taylor, are you responsible for this?"

Miss Rosalie and the rest of the class waited. In the suspended silence Eleanor became aware of the silky sound of wind feathering the sea grass and the faint lapping of waves on the beach a hundred yards away.

At last Nat stifled a nervous laugh and scratched his head. "It was just a joke," he mumbled.

"Step forward for your punishment," Miss Rosalie said.

Nat's worn shoes made scuffing sounds on the wooden floor as he walked to the front of the classroom. He held out a dirty hand with his palm facing up. Eleanor couldn't watch, but just before she squeezed her eyes shut, she saw that Nat was shaking. Then she heard the ruler slap once, softly. Eleanor opened her eyes in surprise. Why, that hadn't even sounded like it hurt. Their old teacher had smacked much harder and sometimes whipped their legs with cedar branches.

"You'll have no recess for one week," said Miss Rosalie in a voice that didn't sound very firm. Nat returned to his desk, and as he came down the aisle, Eleanor heard him mutter something under his breath.

"Mr. Taylor, what did you say?" Miss Rosalie's thin face was scarlet.

"My papa says you're a suffragette," he said loudly, turning around to face her.

"Two weeks without recess! Take your seat, young man!" Miss Rosalie smacked her desk with her ruler.

A few children gasped. What was a suffragette? Eleanor wondered. Something awful, clearly. Otherwise why was Miss Rosalie so upset? Later that morning while working in her *Blue Back Speller* Eleanor pretended she needed to look up a word in the big *Webster*'s dictionary with the thin, crackly pages next to Miss Rosalie's desk.

There it was: "suffragette: a woman advocate of female suffrage." Well, that was no help. What was "suffrage"? Maybe it meant suffering, like having babies or something. Virgie Mae's older sister had had a baby two years ago, and from the women's whispered talk Eleanor was sure she suffered a lot. She quickly found "suffrage," directly above "suffragette."

"Suffrage: the right to vote, especially in a political election."

So a suffragette was a woman who thought women should be allowed to vote. Eleanor returned to her seat.

Over the rest of the morning, as she worked on *Helen's Reading* and *Sandford's Arithmetic*, she thought about this. The dictionary didn't make suffragettes sound bad, but Miss Rosalie sure acted like being called one was. She had taught the class that democracy was a good form of government. If it was good for men to vote, why not women?

"Are suffragettes bad?" she asked Virgie Mae during lunch, as they sat in the schoolyard eating ham biscuits from their lunchpails. They took turns drinking water from a conch shell that was kept by the pump for that purpose. Around the back of the school they could hear Nat chopping wood for the stove in the schoolroom.

Virgie Mae twirled a thin yellow braid around her finger. "Papa says they're hooligans. He says they ought to be lined up and horsewhipped."

"Well, I swan!" Eleanor bit into the fig she had picked from a bush in her sister Iona's backyard. Inside the purplish yellow skin was bright pink fruit.

"And my mother says their behavior is not ladylike," Virgie Mae added, rolling her eyes. Virgie Mae *looked* ladylike—she was delicate and ivory-skinned, with powdery freckles on her face—but she often complained about her mother's many rules.

"What do suffragettes do?" Eleanor pressed Virgie Mae.

"I don't rightly know. Papa says they handcuff themselves to courthouse steps."

"What on earth for?"

"I don't know. And they go on hunger strikes."

"They refuse to eat?" Eleanor thought of the winter nights when Papa didn't catch anything for dinner and wondered why anyone would want to go hungry.

"I believe so." Virgie Mae licked the biscuit crumbs from her fingers, then changed the subject. "I reckon putting a sand crab in your desk must be Nat's way of saying he's sweet on you."

"How can you say such a thing, Virgie Mae Salter?" Eleanor smacked her friend's arm. "Nat Taylor is the biggest bully in Atlantic Grove! I would rather die!"

Virgie Mae's laugh was the long, teasing kind.

After school Miss Rosalie stopped Eleanor on her way out. Virgie Mae waited for her at the edge of the schoolyard.

"Thank you for bringing me the broom earlier today, Eleanor. We don't see sand crabs very often in upstate New York."

"You're welcome, ma'am," said Eleanor. "I've always wanted to know about New York. Why did you leave?"

Miss Rosalie smiled, and when she did that her thin face was pretty. Eleanor wondered if Miss Rosalie felt lonely in their little fishing town. People called Atlantic Grove "the jumping-off place from nowhere" because even though it was on the mainland, the main road was miles away. The only way to get anywhere was by boat. Eleanor felt a kinship with Miss Rosalie. She desperately longed to escape to somewhere exciting.

On the wall behind Miss Rosalie's desk was a map of

North Carolina. If Eleanor held up her thumb and fore-finger and measured, the distance between Atlantic Grove and New Bern—the city where the mailboat landed—was only a few inches. In real life it seemed like a million miles.

"I left because I needed a job. You want to go places, don't you, Eleanor?"

"Yes, of course. Don't you?"

"Atlantic Grove is beautiful. Why are you so anxious to leave?"

"Oh, there's nothing here but sand and yaupon bushes and sea grass, ma'am. Once I took the mailboat over to New Bern, and there were carriages, and automobiles, and ladies with parasols, and streetcars, and baseball games, and picture shows, and every kind of thing that you might ever want to buy!"

"I have a book for you to borrow." Miss Rosalie smiled again and went to her desk. She handed Eleanor a thick, worn book whose cover was a deep shade of blue. Eleanor read the title—*Little Women*. "This is a story about a young woman a lot like you, a young woman who wants something different. Maybe you'll like it."

"Oh, thank you." Eleanor wrapped both arms around the book and held it close to her chest.

Virgie Mae's eyes widened when Eleanor reached the edge of the schoolyard. "Does that book have pictures? Does it show the fashions in New York—the hats and dresses?"

"No. She says it's a story about a young woman who wants something different. Like me, she says."

"I want something different, too," said Virgie Mae with yearning.

On the way home they stopped by Mr. Fulcher's store. Mr. Fulcher kept a shelf of everyday things like flour, beef jerky, fishhooks, thread, and buttons so folks did not have to go to Beaufort or New Bern for them. He also handed out the mail. When the girls came in, Mr. Fulcher grinned and reached under the counter. "I know what you've come for!" he said, waving a colorful postcard. "And I know what Frank's going to buy!"

⤜ *Anywhere but Here* ⤛

Eleanor practically snatched the postcard from Mr. Fulcher. She and Virgie Mae stared at the shiny black automobile pictured on it. Mr. Fulcher leaned across the counter. "That's some snazzy automobile."

Eleanor flipped the card over and read out loud what Frank had written:

Hi Folks!

I have made mountains of money working on the Panama Canal, and am a lucky man not to have come down with yellow fever like so many of the fellows. Believe it or not, the skeeters here are worse than at home. What do you think of this car, Papa? Don't be surprised if I come to visit behind the wheel of one of these!

Respectfully,
your son and brother,
Frank

Eleanor and Virgie Mae stood in Mr. Fulcher's store and reread Frank's words many times. He and Papa had never gotten along, but everyone had still believed Frank would stay and fish with Papa when he finished school. He had tried it for a while, but one day he and Papa had a fight while gigging flounder off Core Banks at low tide. Eleanor never knew what they fought about, but Frank waded home across the shallow sound, tied his clothes in a knapsack, and then hopped aboard the "Mullet Line" train heading due north.

They didn't hear from him until a month later, when they received a postcard from Washington, D.C. He had gotten work as a carpenter in the White House, he wrote, and had actually met President Theodore Roosevelt. "President Roosevelt has more energy than a hooked hammerhead," Frank wrote. "One person told me he does not sleep more than an hour a night. And, Eleanor, his daughter Alice drives an automobile twenty-five miles per hour!"

A year later he sent a postcard from Mexico, saying he had been hired on to help dig the Panama Canal. Eleanor had pored over the atlas at school the very next day to see just where Panama was. She used her finger to trace over the narrow sliver of land where they were digging. It looked wider than the Outer Banks. Her teacher explained that the Panama Canal would save ships the long trip of going all the way around the southern tip of South America.

For more than three years now, Papa had been saying that Frank would soon come home hanging his head with nothing to show for all his talk of adventure and riches.

Eleanor didn't like him saying that. When she was little and Papa was away fishing for days at a time, Frank was the one who put vinegar and soda on her jellyfish stings, who played the harmonica in front of the wood stove, and who read to her from the Sears Catalog while her sisters Iona and Lila did the dishes after dinner. He called her "Little Miss Priss" because her favorite part of the catalog was the section with the stylish dress-up clothes.

"He doesn't ask after any of us, does he?" said Virgie Mae as they continued down the path toward home. "His life sounds awful exciting."

"He has mountains of money and maybe even an automobile," agreed Eleanor. "I bet he'll marry some fancy lady."

Virgie Mae didn't answer. Instead she sighed and kicked a broken oyster shell.

Virgie Mae's weathered house appeared on the inland side of the path just beyond a thicket of twisted yaupon bushes. Her mother was sweeping the stoop.

"See you tomorrow!" Virgie Mae called over her shoulder as she ran toward her house.

Eleanor continued down the dirt path past the fish shack. Some of the fishermen had already come in for the day and were sitting on the dock cleaning fish, but she knew Papa wouldn't be back yet. Her own cottage was past the fish shack, behind the dunes. Eleanor ducked through a gap in the yaupon bushes and crossed the flat, sandy yard. Iona and Lila were taking in the dry laundry. The wind from the sound blew the clothes in wild dancing billows. Iona, her oldest sister, was tall and stern. She was twenty-two, ten years older than Eleanor, and lived across the road with her fisherman husband, Jesse, and two sons, Jesse Junior and Clarence. Lila was fifteen, with the same square face and thick, wavy brown hair as Eleanor, but she was more solidly built and had no-nonsense brown eyes, while Eleanor's were green and dreamy.

"We got a card from Frank!" Eleanor put Miss Rosalie's book on the wraparound wood-plank porch and waved the postcard.

"Just because my little brother has gotten biggety, you won't get out of helping with the wash," Iona said. "Get out here and pull down some of this bed ticking."

Eleanor sighed. She hated chores. It seemed as though her sisters did nothing but work from sunup to sundown.

Lila was going to be married to Caleb Varnam soon. One Saturday Caleb took Lila to the picture show starring Lillian Gish at the Athens Theatre in New Bern. Afterward they went to Bradham's Drugstore and had a Pepsi-Cola, and Caleb asked Lila to be his wife. Eleanor hoped this very thing would happen to her, without the getting married part, that is.

"Don't you want to hear what Frank has to say?" She slid the postcard into her pocket.

Lila handed Eleanor a stiff dry pillow slip to fold. "I already know what he has to say. That he's having wonderful adventures and is making bushels of money. Am I right?"

"Well, not just that." Eleanor put the folded pillow slip into the basket.

"Grab hold of the other end of this bed ticking," commanded Iona.

Eleanor took one end of the dry ticking and helped Iona pull it down from the clothesline. They would stuff dried seaweed inside it to make a fresh mattress.

"I reckon if fishing is a good enough life for Papa and the rest of us," Iona said, " it ought to be a good enough life for Frank."

"Oh, Iona, fishing is no life for a man like Frank." Frank was modern, and he had style. Eleanor could not imagine him spending his life on a fishing boat. "Frank's going to buy a new automobile. What do you think of that?"

"Well, it must be just the cat's meow." Iona shook her head as they folded the ticking.

"Look at the photograph." Eleanor pulled the card out of her pocket and pointed.

Iona took the postcard from Eleanor's outstretched hand and squinted at it. Then she passed it to Lila. "An automobile wouldn't do me much good." Iona jerked her head at her house across the road. "Just as soon have a sharpie." Iona was the only woman in Atlantic Grove who could handle a sharpie and haul fishnets by herself.

Eleanor kept folding clothes and was silent.

"You're mighty quiet. Is our way of life not good enough for you, either, Miss Priss?"

There was no sense in getting Iona all riled up, so Eleanor changed the subject. "Why do you suppose ladies are not allowed to vote?"

Iona shrugged and began unpinning Papa's shirts from the line. "Well, because men get more schooling, I reckon."

"That's not true, Iona. Last spring, when the mullet

started running, Raymond Presley dropped out of school. He was two years older than me, but I knew my multiplication tables much better than he did. And everyone at school knows Nat Taylor can hardly read, but I can read the newspaper."

Without replying, Iona moved down the line to where Jesse's shabby dungarees flapped smartly in the salty breeze. The wooden clothespins squeaked and snapped as she released the homemade clothes.

"Well, the whole idea is just not ladylike," Lila offered. "Politics is men's business."

"Why?"

"Who would take care of the children?" said Iona.

"Lila and I don't have any children."

"Lila will soon enough!"

"Caleb wants four boys, but I want four girls," said Lila. She pulled the clothespins from the waistband of Papa's overalls, then folded them, smoothing her hands over the fabric, worn nearly threadbare.

"I can tell you right now," Iona said, folding Eleanor's faded Sunday dress, "you won't meet yourself a husband at the ballot box."

"I don't want a husband!" said Eleanor. She thought about Nat Taylor putting the sand crab in her desk and how Virgie Mae said he was sweet on her. There was not a boy in Atlantic Grove that she wanted to spend ten minutes with, much less marry.

"Well, what on earth do you want, Eleanor?" Iona looked at her sharply.

Eleanor didn't answer at first. Just over Core Sound,

past a thin sliver of land, was the restless blue-brown Atlantic Ocean, the water whose moods and seasons controlled the lives of everyone she knew. She watched the lazy rhythm of the white sea oats waving over the dunes and the sandpipers running along the water's edge. No one in the family except Frank had ever thought about leaving. But Eleanor did.

"I feel like everything is happening somewhere else—and I'm missing out," she said.

Eleanor helped Iona and Lila fold the rest of their clothes. There wasn't one item stacked in the basket that hadn't been sewn by one of the sisters. She began to think about how lonely life would be once Lila moved into the new house Papa and Caleb were building next-door, especially when Papa was away fishing for three or four days at a time. She thought of herself, old and gray, left behind and living with Papa.

"Lila, once you're married, can I live with you and Caleb?"

"Somebody's got to keep house for Papa," said Lila.

"I have my own family," added Iona. "I can't be checking on the old codger all the time. That leaves you, Eleanor."

Eleanor wished she could forget about Papa and the chores and go somewhere by herself to read the book Miss Rosalie had loaned her. She would not be able to waste kerosene after dinner for such a thing.

"Mr. Fulcher said he'd trade us some buttons and thread for two bags of chopped yaupon," Iona said. The sisters often traded dried yaupon leaves, used for medicinal tea, for items they wanted at Mr. Fulcher's store.

"No one ever got anywhere by chopping yaupon!" Eleanor exclaimed in irritation.

"Suit yourself, Miss Priss. Lila and I will have buttons on our dresses for the wedding and you won't."

Eleanor wanted buttons on her dress, so she sighed, took the kitchen knife Iona handed her, and stood beside the fish bench helping chop the dried yaupon leaves into tiny pieces until the bags were filled. Then she went inside the house, climbed up to the loft, and slid her tea tin from under the bed she shared with Lila. She added the new postcard to her collection.

Eleanor loved poring over Frank's postcards. The card from Washington showed a picture of the White House, and Frank had circled one window to show the room where he had built a mahogany bookcase. There was one from New Orleans showing a riverboat, a card from Florida with a pink flamingo, and one from Mexico with a man sleeping under the biggest hat Eleanor had ever seen.

Eleanor also kept a picture of her mother in the tea tin. She had died in childbirth when Eleanor was only one. The photo was sepia-toned and her mother wore a high-necked white wedding dress with her hair swept up. She had a perfect heart-shaped face, pale skin, and a dreamy sort of smile. On the day of her wedding she was fourteen. Eleanor often studied her mother's image, trying to remember the sound of her voice. But she couldn't remember anything.

Papa didn't like to talk about Mama. When she asked Papa for stories about her, he would say only that she was a real lady and that life as the wife of a waterman had been too hard for her. Nat Taylor's mother, the midwife, told Eleanor that all the women of Atlantic Grove used to gather on her mother's front porch in the afternoons after chores were done and listen to her read romances. Eleanor liked that.

Eleanor had collected other treasures in her tea tin: a shark's tooth, a dried starfish, a conch shell, and a sand dollar. Those she had found down on the beach, next to the fish shack, while waiting for Papa to come home.

Today Eleanor went down to the dock and sat swinging her feet back and forth and read *Little Women* while she waited. The book said that the March girls were poor, yet they had enough to eat, they had bookcases full of books, and they had a big, warm house. They wrote newspapers and acted out plays instead of washing clothes, tending the garden, or cooking. And there was no reference whatsoever to chopping yaupon. It dawned on Eleanor that if the March sisters were poor, then the Hill sisters must be worse than poor, because they sure were worse off.

One by one the fishermen came in, unloaded streaming bushels of flounder and spot from the gunwales of their boats, and sold them to the man in the black suit from the fish factory.

"There's John Hill's girl!" said a fisherman named Charlie Donnell as he tied up to the dock and began unloading.

"Have you seen him?" Eleanor asked. She closed her book and slid it into her apron pocket.

"He's got secret fishing spots, don't tell a single soul. No telling when he'll be back," said Charlie with a wink.

Annis H was one of the last sharpies to sail in. When the sun shone in streams of gold across the sound, the prow of *Annis H* cut through the water, and Eleanor could just make out Papa, with his broad shoulders, handlebar mustache, wet shirt, and brown arms. Eleanor stood and waved, then ran to catch the thick, wet rope Papa tossed her to tie up when he docked.

"Did you catch much, Papa?"

"It'll do for November." Beads of sweat collected on his brow as, one after another, he heaved five brimming bushels of spot onto the dock. The edges of his mustache were stiff with salt. With a practiced flick of his wrist he tossed back into the water a stingray that had gotten caught in his net, then dropped one small spot in a fishpail.

"This here's our supper," he said, handing the pail to Eleanor. She looked down at the cloudy-eyed fish and ran her finger along its cold, rough scales. Papa held up his net. Even though she had helped him mend it only this morning, there were already two new holes.

"Some feller from up north claims he's invented a better fishnet," Papa said. "Got doors on it to hold it open while it drags through the water. If that ain't the most foolish thing I ever heard—a fishnet with doors on it. They expect the fish to knock on the door, then you open it and say, 'Please, do come in'?"

Eleanor giggled. What a joke. She pictured a school of mullet or bluefish knocking politely, and Papa opening the door and escorting them into his net.

"Don't laugh, John," said Charlie. "I seen one of them nets the other day, and you can use them in deep water. That feller from New Jersey caught so many he hired a whole crew to help haul in his nets."

"Five bushels in November. There's nothing wrong with this net of mine," said Papa loudly.

"Sure," said Charlie. "I'm just saying it was interesting to see."

Papa kept folding his net and didn't answer.

Eleanor waited while Papa argued with the man from the factory about the price for the fish. Miss Rosalie had talked to the class about the factory just yesterday. While taking attendance, she had called Gus Slocum's name and received no answer.

"Gus Slocum?" she said again, looking up.

"He went to work at the fish house," volunteered Nat Taylor.

"You mean he's quit school?" Miss Rosalie said in surprise.

"Yes'm."

"Children should not be made to work in the fish house," Miss Rosalie exclaimed.

"He's almost twelve, ma'am," said Nat.

"It's not right for children to stand and work for hours without breaks and be paid only a few pennies a day," Miss Rosalie insisted.

"That's not true," Nat interrupted. "Gus told me he was making one dollar fifty cents a week."

"Well, let's just do the math and see how much he makes," Miss Rosalie said. "How many days does Gus work, Nat?"

"He's off Sundays."

"So he works six days a week. Divide one dollar and fifty cents by six and what do you get?"

Ben Willis raised his hand. "Twenty-five cents, ma'am."

Miss Rosalie nodded and wrote "25 cents" on the board. She turned back to face the class. "Twenty-five cents a day. Now, how many of you think that's a lot of money?"

Eleanor raised her hand, along with every other child in the class. Once in her life she had held two cents in her hand, and that was for selling two bags of chopped yaupon. She watched Miss Rosalie's eyes widen and her face pale when she saw the hands. She put down the chalk. "Gus Slocum ought to be in school, not working in the fish house," she said at last.

Eleanor wondered what it might be like for Gus and the other children who worked in the factory. Sometimes when she helped Papa clean fish, she could keep it up for almost an hour without stopping to shake the cramps out of her fingers. She could chop the head off a fish just like that—chop! And then she knew just where to slide her knife to scrape the fins off. And then, last of all, she'd slide the knife inside and open the fish wide like a book, lifting out the laddered bones. It was kind of fun. But that was partly because she liked helping Papa. She didn't know what it would be like cleaning fish in a dark room, at a dripping table, with other people who weren't even family.

When Eleanor told Papa that Miss Rosalie said the fish house was a bad place, he said he didn't know anything about that and didn't want to know. "Who else is going to buy my fish?" he had said.

Papa and Eleanor followed the path to the house, and as they walked through the gap in the yaupon bushes, Eleanor saw Lila by the stove oiling the heavy black skillet, waiting for them to bring her some fish to fry.

Papa complained about the paltry price he had gotten for his fish. Then he cursed the man from New Jersey for inventing the net with doors on it. Eleanor decided not to mention Frank's postcard that day, because Papa probably would be mad about that, too. Part of her wished she could do something about all the things that made Papa mad, but part of her wished she could fly far, far away and never look back.

Miss Rosalie
Cuts Her Hair

Eleanor went to school about four months a year, during the winter. In the cold months many fish swam south, so Papa didn't take *Annis H* out much. For dinner Lila rationed out vegetables she'd canned and mullet that she'd salted away in a barrel under the house.

During the winter Lila and Eleanor sometimes helped Papa gig flounder in the sound or collect clams to sell. Clamshells were round with crescent-shaped ridges. Papa said you could tell how old the clam was by counting the ridges. The sisters would wade out in the sound and plunge their hands into water so cold their fingers turned bright red and ached. They always saved a few for themselves—there was nothing better on a winter night than clam chowder, except maybe oyster stew.

Every fisherman in Atlantic Grove had his own oyster bed, and so did Papa. When he first claimed the land he put a few oysters in the sound near the house, and over the years they had multiplied. He had a rake and some long wooden tongs that he used to harvest the oysters from the ocean floor.

Papa showed Eleanor how to hit the oyster with a hammer, slide the fish knife into the closed shell at just the right spot, give the knife a quick twist, and pop the shell open. The outside of the oyster's shell was rough and ugly, but the inside looked like a satiny purple pillow for a princess. Papa explained that when a grain of sand or dirt got inside the shell, the oyster covered it with layer after layer of lime, which hardened into a pearl. Once, while helping Papa shell oysters, Eleanor found a pearl slightly larger than the head of a pin.

"Papa, look!" Delighted, she held it in her open palm. "We're rich! You won't have to go out on *Annis H* anymore. Iona can buy material for clothes, and Lila can take time off from the garden and the chores, and we can fix the roof, and I can buy some books!" An entirely new life bloomed in bright colors inside her head.

But Papa only laughed. "Pearls for ladies' necklaces don't grow in North Carolina oysters," he said. "They grow in the tropics. This here pearl is worthless." He tossed it on the sand.

Isn't that the way it is about everything here, Eleanor thought. Even our pearls are worthless. But something made her crawl around on her hands and knees until she found the pearl, ignoring Papa's chuckle. She added it to the treasures in her tea tin.

One day in January Miss Rosalie cut her shiny brown hair in a short bob. She suddenly looked younger and slighter, hardly older than her students. Several times during the day Eleanor noticed her reach up to smooth her bun and then stop in midair.

"Doesn't it look horrible?" Virgie Mae said to Eleanor at recess, as they sat by the water pump with their corn bread. "Mama says a girl's hair is her crowning glory."

Eleanor had always loved Miss Rosalie's bun, so neatly wound and pinned at the back of her head. In fact she had dreamed of having one herself when she grew up, and now her teacher had gone and cut it off.

"I wonder if she really *is* a suffragette," Eleanor said.

"Oh, she can't be," said Virgie Mae. "Our folks would never allow that."

But walking by Miss Rosalie's desk later that day, Eleanor saw a copy of the *New Bern Tribune,* and there on the front page was a picture of suffragettes in white dresses sitting in an automobile in a New York City parade with a banner that read "Right to Vote." Eleanor noticed that the suffragettes had short bobs like Miss Rosalie. The article said there was to be a debate about women's suffrage on Friday night in New Bern between citizens and some men from the North. Someone had underlined the date and time of the debate.

Thinking about that debate made Eleanor's stomach hurt. Miss Rosalie was lending her a new book almost every week. She had now read *St. Elmo, A Girl of the Limberlost, Little Dorrit, The Adventures of Tom Sawyer,* and *The Adventures of Huckleberry Finn.* If Miss Rosalie was a suffragette she might run off to New York and march in a parade or chain herself to the courthouse steps, and then where would Eleanor get her books? Maybe Miss Rosalie didn't care about her students anymore, maybe she cared more about being a suffragette. At the same time, now she seemed filled with energy and purpose instead of being sad, and Eleanor liked that.

That same afternoon Miss Rosalie announced they would study geography down by the water. Carrying her atlas, she marched all fifteen pupils to the beach. They were giddy with the novelty of it, and Eleanor heard Nat Taylor whisper to Ben Willis, "Do you think she's gone crazy?" And Ben Willis said, "Crazy as a loon."

Miss Rosalie gathered them around her where the sand was hard and slightly damp. She opened her book to show the Great Lakes. "Now," she said, "we are going to dig the Great Lakes right here in the sand and watch them fill up with water."

The students dug with gusto, caking wet gray sand under their nails and up to their elbows, while Miss Rosalie stood in the stiff salty breeze, holding the atlas open so they could see the map of the lakes. Eleanor and Virgie Mae worked on Lake Ontario, as far away as they could get from Nat and Ben, who were working on Lake Superior. Cold murky water seeped up from the bottom and slowly filled the holes they had dug. They laughed because tiny sand fleas with smooth speckled shells were hiding in the wet sand, and once the students found them, they tried to hide again, digging as fast as they could.

"Look!" said Ben. "That sand flea's dug all the way to the bottom of Lake Erie!" They all thought this was funny.

"Now you will never forget the shape of the Great Lakes," said Miss Rosalie, "because you have dug them with your own hands." Her short hair blew in the breeze, and Eleanor didn't think she ever *would* forget—either the shape of the Great Lakes or Miss Rosalie, standing so straight and serious on the beach.

The next day Miss Rosalie announced that once a week the class would take a nature walk to collect specimens to study, and time each day would be set aside for reading novels about social issues. She would begin with a book called *Uncle Tom's Cabin* by Harriet Beecher Stowe.

That afternoon Eleanor listened with interest as her teacher began to read about Little Eva and her friendship with a colored man named Uncle Tom. There were no colored people living in Atlantic Grove. Eleanor had only met a colored person once when she was visiting Aunt Velma in New Bern and a woman named Nettie came to the back door selling collard greens.

She looked around the room as Miss Rosalie read. Virgie Mae was sketching a Sunday frock in her composition book, and Nat was carving something inside his desk with his fish knife, not listening at all.

Later that afternoon, Eleanor kicked at oyster shells as she and Virgie Mae walked home down the dirt path. "What's wrong with her?" Virgie Mae complained. "Why are we digging holes in the sand and listening to her read made-up stories?"

Eleanor had loved the geography lesson down on the beach. She'd also loved listening to the novel. Miss Rosalie seemed to be in touch with a new and exciting way of thinking, some great wave of change, and Eleanor wanted to know everything about it. Her biggest fear was that Miss Rosalie would go to the debate on women's suffrage and never come back to the one-room school in Atlantic Grove. But Virgie Mae was her best friend, and Eleanor didn't like arguments, so she kept quiet.

"Why doesn't she teach us things we really need to know, such as how to tie a slipknot, or piece a quilt, or cure a jellyfish sting?" Virgie Mae went on.

"Yes, or how to make corn pone or card cotton," said Eleanor with a touch of bitterness, thinking about how her sisters spent their time.

"Or make blackberry preserves," added Virgie Mae, "or knit a sweater."

"Or how to swim," finished Eleanor quietly. Some of the fishermen in Atlantic Grove knew how to swim, but none of the women did.

"Mama says it's very unseemly for a young lady to go gallivanting around in the water," said Virgie Mae. "But I wish I could."

"I know," said Eleanor crossly. She wished there weren't so many things that were "unseemly" for young ladies. She felt sure that if her own mama had lived she would be more daring than Virgie Mae's. After all, Eleanor's mother used to *read* to all the other women of Atlantic Grove. She treasured her vision of Mama on the porch with the other women seated in a circle around her, perhaps doing their needlework as they listened. In the vision her mother had an indescribably beautiful and melodious voice.

"Do you know something I noticed when Miss Rosalie hugged me today?" confided Virgie Mae as they continued down the path. Miss Rosalie had hugged her because she had, for the first time ever, gotten every sum correct on her math test.

"No, what?"

"Today she wasn't wearing a corset. She was wearing a brassiere." Virgie Mae said the word "brassiere" in a loud, delicious whisper.

Eleanor stared at Virgie Mae, who nodded solemnly. "I swear it."

"I don't believe it."

"You look tomorrow. That's what it was, I'm sure of it. I saw a picture of one in the Sears Catalog at Mr. Fulcher's store. Young ladies in the big cities are wearing them now."

If what Virgie Mae said was true, Miss Rosalie was even more modern and daring than Eleanor had supposed. Neither of Eleanor's sisters had ever worn a corset because they couldn't afford them. Eleanor had seen Lila and Iona wrapping strips of cloth tightly around their breasts before putting on their blouses. It looked mighty uncomfortable.

When Eleanor got home, Lila was making biscuits. The house felt warm and cozy, and Eleanor wanted to forget the things that had been worrying her. She stood at the wooden table and helped Lila roll out the dough and cut the biscuits with the rim of a tin cup.

"Lila," Eleanor asked, "have you ever seen a—" she hesitated, then whispered, "brassiere?"

Lila looked shocked. "Why on earth would *you* want to know that, Miss Priss?"

"No reason."

"Hmmph," Lila said, which meant she knew Eleanor wasn't telling the truth.

"Well, would you wear one, ever?"

Lila put the biscuits in the oven and began wiping left-over flour from the table with a rag. "Iona says brassieres leave very little of a woman's bosoms to the imagination."

"But what do you say?"

Lila hesitated. "If I could afford to pay for one, I'd wear a corset the way a woman ought to. I believe wearing a brassiere would be unladylike."

Did that mean Miss Rosalie was unladylike? Eleanor was confused. To make things worse, Lila stared at her chest, as if thinking of something for the very first time.

Eleanor quickly hunched her back and crossed her arms to hide her small breasts, which had been puffy and sore for some time.

"Eleanor Hill, you stop hunching this minute," said Lila, tossing the floury rag on the table. "Sit up straight. Let me see you."

"No, leave me alone," Eleanor said, hunching further and ducking her head.

"Come on now, Miss Priss, stop this foolishness. Sit up."

Eleanor would not sit up. Instead she crossed her arms more tightly around herself and stuck her lip out at Lila.

"Have it your own way," Lila finally said as she peeked in the oven to check the biscuits. "I was going to show you how to wrap yourself, but if you don't want my help so be it."

Eleanor thought about her small, puffy breasts, about digging the Great Lakes in the sand, about *Uncle Tom's Cabin,* and most of all about the debate on women's suffrage. Waves of emotion that she didn't understand rose up inside her, and she started to cry.

"Lord have mercy, sister!" Lila said, laying her white-floured hand on Eleanor's shoulder. "What on earth is the matter?"

It seemed impossible to describe to Lila the shifting currents of her confused feelings, so Eleanor said the first thing that came to mind. "Miss Rosalie cut her hair!"

A Car Crosses the Water

To Eleanor's great relief her teacher *did* come back after the debate. For several weeks school continued smoothly, with more outdoor geography lessons, nature walks, and chapters from novels. Eleanor scanned the top of Miss Rosalie's desk for further evidence of suffragettes whenever she walked by, but saw nothing more.

Nat Taylor caused some excitement in the first of February when he put a toad in Virgie Mae's desk. Miss Rosalie made him chop wood during recess for a whole week.

One day Eleanor noticed that Adeline Fulcher and the Beasley girls weren't coming to school anymore. Then Miss Rosalie stopped reading *Uncle Tom's Cabin* halfway through without a word of explanation. Eleanor wondered why but didn't dare ask.

School in Atlantic Grove always closed with the approach of spring, when the fish swam up from Florida, and scallops began to grow at a rapid rate. Nets needed tying, and mullet needed cleaning. Children had to help with the work.

On the last day of school Miss Rosalie wore a white

dress, just like the suffragettes Eleanor had seen in news-paper photographs. She had sewn together a palm-sized journal of blank pages for each student, even Nat, and gave each of them a pencil wrapped in pretty paper and curled ribbon.

"I won't be returning to teach here," she said, standing before the class. Her face was pinched, and she would not look at Eleanor. "I will be going out West to Wyoming to teach at a frontier school."

Eleanor's heart squeezed into a knot. Miss Rosalie—leaving! She had known something was wrong. At lunch she asked Virgie Mae if she knew why.

"My folks signed a letter asking her to leave," Virgie Mae answered. "Papa said she was putting a lot of North-ern ideas in our heads, and there wasn't no sense in it." Eleanor's corn bread tasted like sawdust in her dry mouth.

After lunch Miss Rosalie wrote her new address on the board. She showed them Wyoming on the map, a big square near the middle of the United States, and explained that it had been a state for only about twenty years. It would take her almost a week to get there by train.

"I will miss all of you," she said before she dismissed them. "I hope you will continue in your schooling, because only through education can men and women alike grow to be informed citizens and wise leaders."

After the other students left, Eleanor stayed to clean out her desk. Her limbs felt as heavy as wet sand. Miss Rosalie came over and pulled her close. She smelled fresh and clean, like soap. Eleanor was afraid she'd cry, so she let go quickly and turned away.

"If you ever need advice or just want someone to talk to, I would be so pleased if you would write to me," said Miss Rosalie, handing Eleanor a box of onionskin stationery with matching envelopes. "I promise to write back."

"I don't understand why you have to go," Eleanor said in a choked voice. Miss Rosalie was leaving her too soon. She had not yet learned enough from her—about novels, about women's suffrage, or about life.

Miss Rosalie looked at her with kind eyes. "It may not seem so now, but perhaps this is for the best. You know, I don't really fit in here, Eleanor."

Neither do I, Eleanor wanted to say.

Eleanor hated leaving Miss Rosalie inside the schoolroom boxing up her belongings. She was grateful Virgie Mae had waited to walk home with her.

"I wonder what our teacher will be like next year," said Virgie Mae as they started down the path.

Eleanor curled the blue ribbon she had saved from her new pencil around her index finger. "I'm still thinking about how much I'll miss Miss Rosalie."

"I don't know, she acted so crazy lately, and her hair looked awful, and I hated listening to that novel."

Eleanor didn't reply. She decided right then that if she wrote Miss Rosalie, she wouldn't tell Virgie Mae about it. They stopped together at Mr. Fulcher's store to check for postcards from Frank, but there wasn't one. "He said he would send a picture of himself sitting in an automobile," Eleanor said with frustration. "It's been weeks and weeks."

"See you at church Wednesday night," Virgie Mae said

when they reached the thicket of yaupon bushes outside her house. During spring and summer they used to see each other almost every day at the fish shack, but lately Virgie Mae's mama had been saying that it was an "unseemly" place for young ladies.

"Come visit when you can," Eleanor called as Virgie Mae ducked through the bushes. Her thin blond plaits bounced on her back as she skipped through her smooth dirt yard, around the corner of her cottage, and out of Eleanor's sight.

The days without school seemed to blend together. In the mornings, while Lila milked Molly, their cow, Eleanor searched under the bushes and in the tall grass for chicken eggs. Papa made fun of Eleanor because she had named one of their chickens Miss Speckle. He said nobody named their chickens. But Miss Speckle had a real personality— she was the greediest when Eleanor threw out the feed, pushing the other chickens out of the way, and she had the strangest hiding places for her eggs. Eleanor thought she deserved a name.

Before lunch Eleanor helped Lila in the garden. They grew corn, sweet potatoes, squash, pole beans, and okra, and this spring Lila was trying out a brand-new fruit called a tomato. The soil in Atlantic Grove was so dark and loamy that people joked, "Don't drop a seed unless you want it to grow." Some days they canned vegetables and salted mullet for the winter.

In the afternoons, if she had time, Eleanor walked to Virgie Mae's for a visit before she went down to the fish shack to help Papa clean the mullet. And then she came home for supper, which was usually fish and some of the pole beans from their own garden or Iona's.

Some evenings they had supper with Iona and her family. Many evenings Caleb came to visit Lila and sometimes stayed for supper. Caleb was skinny and had sandy brownish blond hair. *Too* skinny in Eleanor's opinion. There wasn't enough meat on him to pinch even a layer of skin over his ribs. He owned one pair of baggy dungarees, which had been patched at least a dozen times. But Lila didn't seem to find much fault with his appearance, and she was the one marrying him after all, so Eleanor kept quiet.

Caleb was a fisherman, too, and he and Papa talked mostly about that. Caleb said he planned to build his own sharpie and paint her a sparkling white, and he was going to name her *Lila V.*

"Hmmph," Lila snorted whenever he said that, but her cheeks turned a deep rose, so Eleanor believed she liked it.

One evening Caleb brought up the new fishnet with the doors on it. "I think that feller from New Jersey is onto something, Mr. John," he insisted to Papa. "How about if you and I rig up something along the same lines and see what we pull in?"

"I pulled in eight bushels today without any fancy net. I'd like you to tell me what's wrong with that." Papa lit his pipe and sucked deeply on the mouthpiece. His sunburned cheeks caved in and puffed out until finally the tobacco inside his pipe bowl glowed orange and circles of smoke rose to the ceiling.

"You're a stubborn man, Mr. John," said Caleb.

"Thank you, I'll take that as a compliment," Papa said, and leaned back in his chair.

"Caleb's just trying to help out, Papa," Lila said, clearing the last of the dishes from the table.

"I don't need any help. I been fishing my whole life," said Papa.

Caleb and Lila exchanged a look. Eleanor kept washing the dishes.

After supper Eleanor and Lila sewed until it grew too dark to see. They were working on Lila's trousseau, the clothes that she would take with her to her new house after she and Caleb were married. The sisters had traded dozens of eggs and bags of chopped yaupon for fabric, yarn, and buttons for undergarments, two dresses, an apron, a shawl, and three pairs of socks. Lila would wear the prettier of the two dresses, made of white muslin, for her wedding. As the date grew closer, sometimes they splurged and lit the kerosene lamp so they could finish in time.

"Will Frank be coming back for the wedding?" Caleb asked one night as he watched Lila and Eleanor stitch.

No one said anything for a long moment, and Caleb looked confused, as if he'd said something he shouldn't have. Papa stared at the floor, sucking on his pipe.

"I don't reckon he'd come this long way," said Lila at last.

Everyone sat in silence for a moment or two longer, until Lila pointed out a place where Eleanor had dropped a stitch.

They hadn't heard from Frank in quite some time, but Eleanor received a letter from Miss Rosalie.

May 2, 1913

Dear Eleanor,

   I do not begin my teaching duties for several months, so I am spending this time traveling and seeing the sights out West. The landscape is much different from where you live. Wyoming has flat, endless deserts and majestic mountains that seem to touch the sky. The country seems to go on forever as far as you can see.

   I have been to visit the Yellowstone Park, and saw the famous geyser Old Faithful. I have also been to see Devil's Tower, a volcanic rock that resembles the stump of a tree thousands of feet tall.

   The people here are used to hardship, just like people in Atlantic Grove. There is nothing elegant about this life! At least the mailboat brings you supplies twice a week. Here we get supplies about once a year! But out here women can vote in local elections. There are many women in Wyoming who own businesses and know how to shoot a rifle. I am learning how to shoot a rifle, too—a young farmer named Daniel is teaching me. I practice by shooting at chalk marks on trees. I miss more than I hit, but I am improving!

   Wish your sister Lila much happiness in her marriage for me. Being a bride is a wonderful dream, but being a wife is a most solemn responsibility.

   I hope you will continue your schooling, Eleanor, and even if your family cannot afford to send you to college, keep reading. You are a pretty and spirited girl, so you will turn many a boy's head. But remember that there will be plenty of *time for young men later. Be industrious, independent, and studious, and you will find your chosen path.*

Your devoted teacher,
Rosalie Adams

Eleanor carried the letter in her pocket and reread it often. She tried to picture Miss Rosalie shooting a rifle. Or wearing a fringed jacket and riding chaps, like pictures she'd seen of Annie Oakley.

It took some planning for Eleanor to reply to Miss Rosalie. When Lila sent her to Mr. Fulcher's store for supplies, she took him some eggs, then dusted and arranged the shelves and mopped the floor in exchange for a two-cent stamp. She wrote her reply early one morning after Papa left for the fish shack and Lila was still asleep, smoothing the thin paper and forming her letters with great care.

May 21, 1913
Dear Miss Rosalie,

Your life sounds very exciting. I can't imagine what it must be like to shoot a rifle! I wonder that this is the same United States. Life out West sounds so very different from ours.

All the talk in our family now is about Lila's wedding. Many thanks for your good wishes. I understand what you mean about marriage being a solemn responsibility. Lila is determined to make Caleb a good wife, so I am sure that she

will. She is a hard worker and is well suited to be the wife of
a waterman. I do not believe it would suit me.

I wish I could keep up with my reading, but books are
hard to come by. Could you, if it's convenient, write and
describe the ending to Uncle Tom's Cabin?

Your faithful student,
Eleanor Hill

When she was out in the garden with Lila, Eleanor passed the time imagining Miss Rosalie's life in Wyoming and Frank's life in Panama. She couldn't believe Lila and Iona didn't care about such adventures, that they both were perfectly happy to keep on living right here, watching their husbands sail off before dawn, just like Papa, and spending mornings doing chores and afternoons chopping yaupon and cleaning fish.

"Women out West can vote. And shoot rifles," Eleanor told Lila one morning as they walked down the rows of pole beans, filling their aprons.

"Where have you gotten such crazy ideas?" asked Lila.

"The newspaper," Eleanor lied.

Lila furrowed her forehead and pursed her lips but didn't say anything. She tossed another pole bean into her apron.

Just then there was a commotion down by the dock. Eleanor had never seen so many people there, not even the day Ben Willis's father caught the seven-foot hammerhead shark off Harkers Island. A small crowd was watching the mailboat approach, towing behind it a flat-bottom skiff with a brand-new automobile. The automobile, bobbing on the waves, shone black and square in the sun. Resting his hand on the hood was a tall man in a white suit. Suddenly the skiff rolled over a wave, and the hood of the car flashed so brilliantly that Eleanor was almost blinded. "Well, I swan!" she said.

"Isn't that the ugliest thing you ever saw?" observed Lila.

"No, it's beautiful." The car vibrated with a kind of modern energy that Eleanor liked.

At that moment Iona ran out her front door with a dishtowel in her hand. "What on earth is that?" Her sons, six-year-old Jesse Junior and five-year-old Clarence, came from behind her and shot barefoot through the yard.

A few people had gotten in their boats and rowed over to look. When the man cranked up the automobile and drove it up the hill toward the three sisters, Iona's boys snaked behind like the tail on a kite. When the automobile backfired, with a sound like a gunshot and a puff of oily smelling smoke, they hung back for only a few seconds.

"Lila!" Eleanor cried as the man drove up and stepped from the car. "It's Frank!" She let the pole beans in her apron rain to the ground and ran down the hill to meet her brother. Iona's hand flew to her mouth. Lila shook her head and slowly bent down to pick up the beans.

"Frank!" Eleanor threw herself into his arms. She didn't care if she *did* get garden dirt on his store-bought white suit. This handsome sophisticated man—her own brother! She could hardly believe it. With a big laugh Frank swung her around the way he always had, then grabbed his back, pretending to be in great pain.

"Whoa, Miss Priss, I believe you've outgrown me over the past four years!"

Frank had come home! Eleanor made sure she sat next to him at dinner that night. His olive skin was deeply tanned from working in the sun. His suit looked so beautiful that she wanted to touch it. Eleanor had always loved Frank's graceful hands—she had spent many hours watching his long, patient fingers as he did carpentry work. Papa used to say Frank's hands looked like he'd never done a day's work in his life, but they did now. They were still long and graceful, but they'd grown rough and calloused, too.

"Frank, did you drive that automobile all the way from Panama?" Lila asked, standing at the head of the table with the teakettle.

"Oh no," said Frank. "I took the train. I stopped in to see Aunt Velma and Uncle Owen in New Bern, and that's where I bought it. Isn't it the cat's meow?"

"Oh yes!" said Eleanor, but she noticed that Lila and Papa didn't answer.

"If you don't mind my asking," said Papa, "how much does a contraption like that cost?"

"It's an automobile, not a contraption," said Frank. "And it cost six hundred dollars."

Lila gasped and almost dropped the teakettle on the floor. Papa grunted in disapproval. "You must be rich," said Eleanor.

"I won't lie to you. A man who's not afraid of danger can make a bundle of money working on the Panama Canal," Frank said. "I was smart and enterprising, and they made me a foreman. A good number of the men plan to go to California next. It's the land of milk and honey."

Frank began to talk about the rolling vineyards of California and the breathtaking vistas of the Pacific Ocean. He talked about how everybody in San Francisco was getting rich, and how a man named Levi Strauss had become a millionaire just by making sturdy work britches. "Everything is bigger than life there," he finished.

"I guess bigger must be better," said Lila, slapping a fried mullet onto Frank's plate. "I hear San Francisco is a godless place with every temptation, from gambling to whiskey. It's no place for good Christian men."

"Now, Lila, do I look like a godless man to you?" Frank asked, smiling. "Your cooking smells as good as ever."

"Hmmph," said Lila.

"If you're so all-fired anxious to get to California," said Papa, "why stop here?"

Frank's face reddened, then he cleared his throat. "I was just thinking about y'all, that's all. I wanted you to see my Model T. Thought you'd be proud of me making foreman, Papa."

Papa cleared his throat and used a wooden match to tamp down the tobacco in his pipe.

"I saved every one of your postcards," Eleanor said to break the silence. "The picture of the automobile you sent looks so very . . . modern!"

"The automobile business is the wave of the future, Miss Priss," said Frank with a smile. "Soon everyone will have one."

"That's impossible," said Papa. "They're too expensive. Besides, they're loud and ugly."

"The price will come down, Papa. My Model T was put together in ninety-three minutes, on a conveyor belt. I predict in twenty years you won't see a single horse on Front Street in New Bern, only automobiles."

"I never heard of such foolishness," said Papa. He had finished his dinner and pushed his plate away.

"You wait and see."

"Will you teach me to drive the car, Frank, while you're here?" asked Eleanor.

"No, he will not!" said Papa immediately. "I forbid it."

Everyone was silent. Frank touched her arm and said, "You want to go places, don't you, Miss Priss?" Eleanor, close to tears, nodded. Lila began clearing dishes, and Papa busied himself lighting his pipe.

"Well, Lila," said Frank, "I must have come home at the right time. I hear there's to be a wedding."

Lila blushed and began to talk about the plans. Eleanor wasn't listening. Instead she studied Frank, every dark curl, the squareness of his jaw, the grace of his hands. He had come home, he really had come home. And maybe, just maybe, when he went to California he would take her with him.

⪥ Eleanor ⪦
Disobeys Papa

Eleanor sat in the driver's seat of the Model T. She stretched her neck to see over the steering wheel and through the small rectangular windshield. She stretched the toes of her right foot toward the brake, and the toes of her left toward the clutch. Her left arm was stretched out beside the steering wheel, grasping the hand lever, and her right hand gripped the steering wheel itself.

"Comfortable?" Frank, sitting next to her, asked with a smile.

Eleanor couldn't answer. She was too stretched to speak.

Papa had gone up the Neuse River the day before on a two-day trip. Frank had surprised Eleanor at breakfast that morning by offering her a driving lesson, saying with a wink, "What Papa doesn't know won't hurt him." Eleanor had ignored Lila, who warned repeatedly that what they were planning was bound to incur the worst end of Papa's wrath. Now Lila was in the yard, supposedly scrubbing clothes against the washboard, but she had stopped all pretense of work and stood watching them. Eleanor caught a glimpse of Iona's stern face peering out her doorway across the road. "Papa is bound to find out about this, Frank!" she shouted.

"Not unless you tell him!" Frank shouted back with a grin. "And if you do, you are a kill-joy!"

Lila suddenly smiled. "Eleanor, don't you look a sight!"

"Why, thank you kindly!" Eleanor said, imitating a highfalutin New Bern lady.

In the two days since Frank had come home, Eleanor had watched every time he started the car. She had a general idea of what to do, she just wasn't sure what order to do it in.

"First thing you do," Frank said, "is push the spark up." He indicated a tiny lever on the left side of the steering wheel. "Then open the throttle about five or six notches." He pointed to a lever on the right side of the steering wheel. "Then pull back the hand lever." He pointed to the long lever extending from the floor by Eleanor's left leg, and she pulled it back.

"Next you crank the engine," Frank said, getting out. "Let me show you how." Eleanor slid out and stood in front of the car beside him. "Now, crank it clockwise from bottom to top two or three times. This sends the gasoline up to the engine. Don't grab it straight on, though. Be sure to curl your hand underneath, sort of cradle it. Otherwise it could fly back and break your arm."

Eleanor cradled the crank and did as Frank said. "Good. Now get back in the driver's seat. Keeping your foot on the clutch pedal, gradually open the throttle."

When Eleanor did as her brother instructed, the car started up with a sound like a gunshot and began vibrating so hard it made everything else that had happened so far in her life seem to be in slow motion. Frank saw the look of wild joy on her face and grinned.

"Now push the hand lever forward and lightly press down on the clutch. Then gradually release the clutch and partially close the throttle to go into high speed."

"All right," she said, trying not to sound doubtful about being able to do all that at once.

She found that if she slid down on the slick black leather seat a bit she was less stretched, and could just see the tops of the silky-eared corn in their garden through the space between the dashboard and the steering wheel. She was too short to see the dirt road ahead of her.

She applied light pressure to the clutch but forgot to push the hand lever forward. The car growled like an angry tiger, vibrating enough to scramble her brains, it seemed, but it did not move forward. Miss Speckle, their greedy hen, squawked and ran behind Lila for cover.

"You need to release the emergency brake by pushing the hand lever forward," said Frank.

"Oh!" Eleanor quickly pushed it forward. The car bucked once, like a wild pony. Then the engine died, releasing a foul-smelling puff of oily black smoke.

"Uh ... gradually," Frank added. Eleanor had pictured herself speeding down the road like Alice Roosevelt at twenty-five miles per hour, her braids flying out behind her. This was harder than she thought. "Hold your horses, I've got to restart it." Frank moved the hand lever back to neutral, then went around to the front of the car to crank again.

"You could have hitched up a dozen wagons or walked

there and back by now!" shouted Lila, who was rinsing the lye soap from the clothes in a bucket of well water.

"Kindly hush up," muttered Frank under his breath. "Just about got it!" he called.

"I wish I had me a Kodak!" Iona shouted, now standing in her front yard with a broom. "They could put you on the front page of the *New Bern Tribune.*"

"I bet I'll be the first girl to drive in Atlantic Grove!" Eleanor shouted back. After making a grinding and chugging noise, the car began vibrating once more. She firmly pressed the clutch while pushing the hand lever forward. With a leap, the car started off down the road. Miss Speckle screeched and ran right in front of it, flapping her useless wings every few steps.

"Slow down!" shouted Frank, who had not gotten back in the car. He was running along beside her, grabbing at the door. Eleanor could hear the laughter of her sisters behind her.

"I don't know how!" she shouted back, tearing down the road. She left Frank standing in the dust, out of breath. Her hair was flying out behind her, and the wind was whipping her face, bringing tears to her eyes. What would Miss Rosalie think if she could see her now?

Suddenly Eleanor saw Mr. Fulcher approaching in his wagon, pulled by Millie, his ill-tempered mule. Mr. Fulcher tried to maneuver the wagon to the side of the road, but when Millie saw the automobile she rolled her eyes and reared up on her hind legs with a loud whinny.

Eleanor didn't know what to do. First, by accident, she let the clutch all the way out, putting the car in high gear, and, to her horror, went even faster. Then, in a panic, she pulled back on the hand lever and jammed down on the pedal on the far right that Frank had said was the brake.

The car screeched to a halt and died. Eleanor was almost thrown out.

"Whoa, Millie, whoa girl!" shouted Mr. Fulcher, as Millie left the road completely and shied right through the middle of Lila's garden, pulling the wagon behind her.

"Lord have mercy!" Eleanor heard Lila shouting from the yard. "Look at my butter beans!"

"Ellie, are you all right?" Frank ran up and leaned on the hood, catching his breath.

"I think so," Eleanor said in a trembly voice.

"Whew. That was a close one. Maybe this isn't such a good idea."

"Oh no, Frank, don't give up on me yet. Please."

Frank pushed his damp hair back from his brow. He leaned against the hood, taking deep breaths.

"Mr. Fulcher, I swan," they heard Iona saying. "What have you done to my sister's okra?"

Eleanor spotted a fluffy speckled tail disappearing down the road. "Miss Speckle's getting away!"

Frank grinned. "Why, we can't let a chicken get the better of an automobile, can we, Miss Priss?" He went through the crank routine all over again, and the engine caught. This time Eleanor gave Frank a chance to jump in, and then managed to coordinate the hand lever, the clutch, and the throttle with steady confidence.

"Good, good," he said as they chugged down the road.

They were gaining on Miss Speckle, who suddenly veered onto a footpath and started trotting down the beach. It was low tide and the sand was packed down smoother than any road.

"What do you think?" Eleanor glanced at Frank, who shrugged and grinned.

"Follow that chicken!"

She steered the car, with much jolting, onto the footpath that led to the hard-packed sand. And that was how Eleanor found herself driving Frank's automobile straight down the beach, racing after a chicken.

Eleanor thought, Let me never forget this moment, this day when I first drove a car. She wished she could put the memory in her tea tin and be able to feel the thrilling sensation every time she opened it.

Soon they were both damp with fine salt spray and wet sand, and Miss Speckle, with a squawk of exhaustion, ran into a thicket of sea oats. "She'll find her way home," Frank said with a laugh, and Eleanor drove right by her.

They drove up and down the beach for more than an hour, until Eleanor mastered the rhythm of starting and driving the car. She even practiced using the middle pedal, which was reverse.

"You're a good driver," Frank said at last.

"Do you really think so?" Pleased, Eleanor moved over to the passenger seat and let him drive home. She watched the landscape of the dunes and the water slide by, then turned around and saw imprints in the sand seem to roll off the tires as they drove down the beach. She had a powerful feeling that life in Atlantic Grove, which had been a certain way for many years, was about to change. Some people, like Papa and Iona and Lila, didn't want anything to change. Others, like Frank and herself, would welcome it. But change was coming, no matter what anybody did.

When they got back home, Mr. Fulcher was helping Iona and Lila repair the garden. Millie stood under the live oak grazing and was only mildly startled to see the car again. Miss Speckle was under the front stoop, her beak buried in her wing.

"Shame on you, Frank Hill, for scaring my Millie!" said Mr. Fulcher from between two rows of flattened butter beans as Frank and Eleanor climbed stiffly out of the Model T.

"I wasn't driving!" Frank protested.

"Look at you two!" Iona said. "You'd think you've been swimming in a mudhole!"

Frank and Eleanor looked at each other. It was true. Dust, sand, and salt spray were caked in a fine layer on every inch of them. They both laughed. "I don't care!" Eleanor threw her arms in the air. "Because now I know how to drive a car!"

"You'll care soon enough if Papa gets wind of this," said Iona.

Eleanor's stomach did a flip. She and Frank had blatantly disobeyed Papa. A wave of nausea swept from her stomach to her throat.

Frank glanced up from the pump, where he'd been using his handkerchief to wash the salt from his face and neck. "You don't plan on telling him, do you, Iona?"

Iona held her back very straight and for a long moment her eyes bored a hole through Frank. "I reckon not," she said. Her thin mouth slowly curved upward, just a little.

By late afternoon they had packed the black dirt around the bruised plants and pruned the broken stalks. The rows in the garden looked as neat as ever. But they had the biggest mess of butter beans to shuck that Eleanor had ever seen. Lila dumped them into her apron. "Seeing as how this is all your doing, you and Frank can shuck these butter beans, Miss Priss."

Eleanor and Frank stood by the fish bench in the backyard and shucked butter beans for the rest of the afternoon. "Here I am, a man of the world," Frank said, skimming a row of shiny green butter beans from their hull with the flat of his thumb. "I've helped build a bookshelf for President Teddy Roosevelt in the White House. I've been foreman to a hundred men building the Panama Canal. I've bought my own Model T. I come home for a visit and do they give me a parade? No. I'm shucking butter beans."

Eleanor touched her brother's arm. "I would give you a parade."

He smiled. "We're alike, you and I. We think there's more to life than what's here."

"How long will you stay, Frank?"

Frank looked out over the sound. "I'll stay and see Lila married."

Eleanor silently counted the days. Fourteen. That was how long she'd have him.

By the time Papa got home that night, there was a big pot of butter beans on the stove and neighbors on either side were cooking butter beans, too. Eleanor thought she and Frank had covered their tracks but knew something was wrong when Papa threw his muddy hip-waders on the porch, instead of standing them by the door, and let the screen door slam behind him. Had Mr. Fulcher told?

"Frank Hill," he growled, "I thought I was seeing things." He tossed a bucket with two mullet at Lila. "I came back down the river early and was out on the water when, lo and behold, with my own eyes I seen Eleanor driving that car of yours down the beach! I said to myself, this couldn't be true, because I forbade her doing it! People from here to Raleigh will be talking about that wild girl Eleanor Hill." He slapped his pipe and tobacco on the table. "Frank, don't you have the sense God gave you? Letting that girl drive a car down the beach?"

Eleanor blushed. She had driven up and down the beach like a hooligan, and Papa had seen the whole thing.

Frank, sitting at the table, looked up from the butter beans Lila had just set in front of him. "There's no reason she shouldn't learn how to drive, Papa."

"I said it was forbidden. That's reason enough."

"She's a good driver."

"Papa, don't blame him," Eleanor said.

Papa wasn't listening. He was staring at Frank. "I'd like to take you, Frank Hill, and your Model T, and your fine clothes, and your highfalutin ideas, and throw you off the end of the pier!"

Eleanor and Lila exchanged wide-eyed looks. Eleanor was the one who had driven the car, yet it was Frank whom Papa was mad at. Papa looked for reasons to get mad at Frank. It wasn't fair.

Frank took a deep breath. "I guess it's too much to ask that you might be *proud*."

Papa sat down at the table with a loud thump. "Proud of what? Pie-in-the-sky ideas?" Lila served him a plate of mullet and butter beans without a word. He tucked his napkin in his belt. "Eleanor, you're to go to bed with no dinner."

"Yessir." She hung her head.

"Lila, this is the biggest mess of butter beans you've ever give me."

Lila had the good sense not to answer.

"And, Frank," Papa said, jabbing the air with his fork, "every day you sleep under my roof, you'll pull your weight. You can come out and haul fishnets on *Annis H* tomorrow like the rest of us."

Frank stood up. "If it's money you want from me, take it." He reached in his pocket and threw a folded bill and some coins on the table. "Here. I've got plenty of it. I was a success in Washington and in Panama and I will be in California, too. I don't have to come here and listen to insults." He grabbed his coat from the hook beside the door and stalked out.

The silence left behind was so heavy Eleanor couldn't breathe. Papa, shoveling butter beans into his mouth, seemed oblivious. He swiped the money to the floor, then turned his glittering eyes on her. "I told you to go to bed."

Eleanor climbed to the loft and lay down on the bed. Her heart was aching so much that she barely noticed the growling of her stomach. She would never eat another butter bean as long as she lived. She lay awake long after

Lila came up to bed and Papa lay snoring in his bedroom downstairs, straining her ears for Frank.

He was going to leave again. She knew it. Finally she crawled out of bed, very quietly, so as not to disturb Lila, and tiptoed downstairs to the doorway. She peered through the thick mosquito screen out into the yard. The inky hulk of the Model T was still there under the live oak. A dark figure sat on the hood, taking swigs out of a tall bottle.

"Frank!" she hissed. He looked up, and she waved. He put the bottle out of sight and slid silently to the ground. With unsteady footsteps, he climbed the porch steps, skipping the second one, which they both knew creaked.

"You're going to get us all in trouble, Miss Priss." Eleanor could smell his sweet whiskey breath through the screen.

"Please stay until Lila's married," she whispered. "Promise."

Frank regarded her silently, then nodded. "I'll try. Now, go to sleep."

"Where will you sleep tonight?"

"In my car, I reckon."

On the way down he forgot to skip the squeaky step and they both flinched, but Papa's snoring didn't waver. Frank crossed the yard and threw one leg over the back door of the Model T. He slid into the backseat and disappeared from Eleanor's view.

The Things Nobody Talked About

After one night in the car, Iona offered Frank a pallet at her house. A few nights later he moved back to Papa's house, where Papa resumed speaking to him in short necessary sentences such as "Pass the collard greens" or "The roof shingles need fixing." Eleanor silently counted each day that passed. Her excitement about Lila's wedding was dampened with the knowledge that Frank would leave when it was over.

Lila and Eleanor had sent a handwritten invitation to Uncle Owen and Aunt Velma using their very best penmanship. It read:

> *Mr. John Hill requests the pleasure of your company*
> *At the wedding of his daughter Lila Hill*
> *To Caleb Varnam*
> *Saturday, June 14, 1913, at two-thirty in the afternoon*
> *The Church of Two Hundred Trees, Atlantic Grove, North Carolina*

While helping sew Lila's trousseau, Eleanor thought with dread and curiosity about Lila and Caleb sleeping together in the same bed as man and wife. Iona said a woman's duty to lie with her husband was described in the Bible. To Eleanor's mind a "duty" was like a chore, something you had to do but didn't like, such as making lye soap or scrubbing pots. When she was five or six, she caught a peek through the slightly open bedroom door of Iona sitting on Jesse's lap and kissing him. Iona did not act like kissing Jesse was a duty. But that was a different Iona, an Iona before two children and her belly growing round with what Lila said was another baby on the way. Now Iona pulled away when Jesse tried to peck her cheek or slide his arm around her waist. Maybe she figured her duty was done and didn't want to bother with kissing anymore.

Eleanor and Virgie Mae had once discussed where babies came from after Molly had her new calf. "Mama told me Bossie found her calf out in the pasture," said Virgie Mae. "And she said babies come in flour barrels. They grow over the winter in the root cellar. Do you believe that?"

"I don't know," said Eleanor.

"But I remember that Papa took Bossie to visit Mr. Willis's bull back in the fall, and it wasn't long after that she started looking fat."

"Hmm," said Eleanor. "Papa took Molly to visit Mr. Willis's bull, too."

No one had ever bothered to tell Eleanor where babies came from, even a made-up story. No one in her house ever discussed it at all. But she had noticed that the rooster nearly crushed the hens when they were mating, and sometimes the hens would run when they saw him coming.

And mating dragonflies appeared to be glued together and performed a looping intricate dance among the cattails.

"Papa wouldn't let me watch when Bossie had her calf, but I peeked in the barn and saw its legs coming out of her rear end," Virgie Mae said.

"Really?" Eleanor stood rooted to the road.

"And then Bossie licked it all over, blood and all."

"Ugh!" Eleanor felt sick.

"I suppose that's what a good mother cow ought to do," said Virgie Mae thoughtfully.

Eleanor sighed. She tried to imagine husbands and wives wrestling together or babies coming out of mothers. The idea was too horrifying to talk about. Which was probably why no one ever did.

The day before Lila's wedding the sea oats seemed to stand still and radiate heat. The white sand was blinding in the hot sun. The sound shifted glassy, brownish and warm as water in a washtub.

Aunt Velma and Uncle Owen arrived on the mailboat late that morning. Velma was Eleanor's mother's older sister, and she had promised to help her nieces prepare for the wedding. She was an expert seamstress and would put the finishing touches on Lila's dress.

Aunt Velma ran up the porch steps, holding out her plump, loose arms. Uncle Owen followed, carrying a Victrola he had brought in honor of the occasion. They had also brought Uncle Owen's niece Gertrude, a stylish-looking girl with spit curls who was staying with them and helping Aunt Velma with her sewing.

"There you are!" cried Aunt Velma. "It's hot enough to fry an egg on the dock. I must get a hug from this beautiful bride. Frank, don't you look the dandy, with those store-bought britches and pointy shoes!" Frank turned around, grinning, so she could get a look at him.

"And, Eleanor, you look so much like your mama when she was your age! I wish she could see you." Eleanor let Aunt Velma fold her in her arms. "Before we know it, you'll be getting married, too, child!"

"But I don't want to get married!"

"Don't be silly, of course you do, every girl wants to get married." Aunt Velma brushed a stray hair back from Eleanor's forehead.

"Aunt Velma, I wish we didn't have to use an outhouse while we're here," said Gertrude, wrinkling her nose.

"Idle wishes cannot fill dishes," intoned Uncle Owen. Frank winked at Eleanor. Uncle Owen had always quoted old sayings, and once Frank joked that he wondered if Uncle Owen ever said anything that he had thought up himself.

"May we please listen to the Victrola?" Eleanor eyed the black cylinder and the box with the crank and turntable under her uncle's arm.

"Yes, let's," said Frank. "I say we crank up this machine right now."

Uncle Owen, short and heavyset but quick on his small feet, promptly set down the Victrola and held aloft the black cylinder. Gently he placed it on the Victrola and cranked the handle. "The great Caruso," he announced.

And that was how Eleanor, Iona, and Lila cleaned the

house, to the soaring tenor arias of Enrico Caruso, whom Uncle Owen described as the greatest opera singer of all time. They scrubbed the wood-plank floor and swept the yard smooth, then scoured the cottage windows with vinegar and water as Caruso's high, ringing notes stilled the air.

Aunt Velma had brought a tablecloth and a silver serving piece to cut the cake, which Eleanor polished until she could see her upside-down face. Caruso was the only music Uncle Owen had for the Victrola, and after he had played it three times, Aunt Velma asked him to stop. Eleanor noticed that while the others cleaned, Gertrude went on several strolls around Atlantic Grove with Frank.

Meanwhile Aunt Velma had settled in a rocker on the porch with Lila's dress draped over her knees. "Mercy, you don't get decent light inside your cottage for sewing," she said to Eleanor, working a delicate lacy pattern around the collar and sleeves of the wedding dress with tiny, even stitches.

"How do you do that?" Eleanor asked.

"Oh, there's nothing to it. I could teach you in no time." Aunt Velma stopped to knead her swollen fingers. "You know, I'll need someone to help me after next year. Gertrude will finish high school and go for her teacher training."

Later, while Aunt Velma stood by the stove using flatirons to press Lila's dress, the three sisters rolled out the dough for four blackberry pies and mixed the eggs and flour for the pound cake.

Uncle Owen had brought four bottles of Pepsi-Cola that cost five cents each from New Bern to serve after the wedding. Mr. Bradham, a New Bern pharmacist, had come up with the recipe for Pepsi-Cola fifteen years before, and it became so popular he decided to produce it full-time. Pepsi-Cola wasn't something you drank every day, unless you were rich, and Lila was thrilled to have some for her wedding. Besides, as Lila pointed out, the night they got engaged, she and Caleb had split a Pepsi-Cola, so it had a special meaning to them.

Pepsi-Cola was better with ice in it, of course, and tomorrow Papa and Frank would go get a block from the fish house so the guests could shave some off and drop it in their glasses.

Late in the afternoon, before the mosquitoes came out, Papa, Frank, and Uncle Owen took bars of lye soap down to the sound to bathe. Eleanor and Lila brought in buckets of water from the well, heated it on the cookstove, and filled the metal bathtub. They were dead tired.

"I could soak in here all night." Eleanor lay her head back against the side of the tub when it was her turn and let the warm water cover her up to her neck.

"The cake is pretty, isn't it?" Lila was lathering her hair.

"It rose up real nice."

"And my dress looks elegant, doesn't it?" Lila added.

"I like Aunt Velma's fancy stitching."

"And the silver looks awful pretty, doesn't it?"

"Awful pretty." Eleanor studied Lila's face. "You aren't nervous, are you?" Lila had always seemed so sure of herself. She didn't question things as Eleanor did.

"Well..." Lila's eyes met Eleanor's. "A wedding is supposed to be the most perfect day in a girl's life. A dream come true."

Eleanor thought that everything about the wedding *was* perfect—the dress, the cake, the pies, the silver, the tablecloth—everything except Caleb. Caleb was perfectly nice, but his pants were too baggy and his Adam's apple stuck out too much and he could never think of a clever thing to say. He was simply too *ordinary* to be a groom. But Eleanor couldn't tell her sister that.

"Everything *is* perfect, Lila. Tomorrow will be perfect."

Lila handed Eleanor a towel, and she stood up in the tub and wrapped it around herself. Just then Aunt Velma, who had returned from taking Gertrude to visit with Iona, knocked on the door and poked her head in.

"Lila, Eleanor, I made something for you. Gertrude wanted one, so I made three. I copied the pattern straight from the Sears Catalog. *All* of the stylish ladies in New Bern are wearing them." She handed them two white boxes, her mouth pinched in an effort not to smile.

Lila and Eleanor exchanged puzzled looks, then opened their boxes. Each held a blousy cotton shirt with thin straps and tucks around the waist. Lila's was larger than Eleanor's.

"What are these?" Eleanor finally asked.

"Why, brassieres, girls! I won't peek while you're trying them on. You just tell me if they fit." She shut the door and went back out on the porch.

"Lord have mercy!" Eleanor dropped her jaw, and they both began to giggle.

"Papa would have a hissy fit." Lila put the straps over her shoulders. She turned her broad back to Eleanor. "Here, button me up."

"I thought you said proper ladies should wear corsets," Eleanor said, struggling with the last of three buttons down Lila's back.

"Well, I am shocked, Eleanor, I really am." She turned around. "How does it look?"

Eleanor clapped her hand over her mouth. She was used to seeing Lila with her breasts wrapped, pressed flat against her rib cage, as if they weren't there at all. The brassiere allowed them to poke out naturally. She giggled.

"What's so funny? Try yours on. It's high time you wore something more than an undershirt."

Eleanor reluctantly slid the thin white straps over her shoulders and turned around for Lila to button the back.

"Stand up straight," Lila said. "Turn around, let me see."

Embarrassed, she turned back around and allowed Lila to pull and adjust the brassiere until she was happy with the fit.

Just then Aunt Velma poked her head back in. "Oh, look, they fit like gloves. I'm tickled to death. You must promise me you'll wear them to the wedding."

"Aunt Velma, I don't know . . . ," Lila began.

"Lila Hill, not another word. I insist. No one is going to look more stylish than my nieces, you hear?"

As soon as Aunt Velma left, Eleanor and Lila slid into their nightgowns. Lila folded the brassieres and put them back in their boxes.

They had given the loft bedroom to Aunt Velma and Gertrude. Uncle Owen was to sleep in Papa's room, and Papa and Frank had gone to Iona's. Eleanor and Lila were to share a mattress in the main room next to the cookstove. They kicked off the sheet because of the heat, and both lay without moving, staring at the ceiling. Through the open window came night sounds, occasional voices, and a breath of a cool breeze.

Eleanor's mind was abuzz. She would never sleep.

"Lila, are you awake?"

"Um-hmm."

"Are you going to wear the brassiere?" The two boxes were sitting by the stove.

"I just don't know."

"I will if you will."

Lila hesitated. "Oh, all right," she finally said. They lay in silence for a few minutes.

"This is the last night we'll sleep together," Eleanor said. "Tomorrow night you'll be sleeping with Caleb."

"I reckon that's so," Lila said after a minute.

"Have you ever given Caleb a kiss?"

Lila didn't answer for a long time. Eleanor thought she had fallen asleep.

"Once I did, after church, behind the dunes, when everyone else was having a picnic. We were already engaged, of course."

"Did you like it?"

"Mercy, what kind of question is that?"

"Well, did you?"

"I did, a little." Then Lila added, "Want me to tickle your back?"

"All right," said Eleanor. She turned over, and Lila gently swirled her fingertips over her back. Because her hands were so strong and rough, Eleanor was always amazed her touch could be so light.

They lay there for a long time. Eleanor was full of questions. Was Lila afraid to sleep in the same bed as Caleb? Was she afraid of having babies? After all, their mama had died having one.

But Lila's fingertips kept swirling, swirling, ever so lightly. She stopped herself from thinking that tomorrow her sister would be doing her "wifely duty" with Caleb or that Caleb would even ask it of her. She dreamed of skimming across the sound with Frank and his Model T on a flat-bottom skiff. And then she spiraled toward sleep.

≈ Lila's ≈
Wedding Day

It was hot as blazes the day of Lila's wedding. Eleanor and Lila got ready together, in the downstairs bedroom, with Aunt Velma running in and out and fussing over every little thing. Eleanor wore a blue flowered gingham dress that had once been Lila's, with puffy sleeves, a large white square collar, and a skirt that fell to midcalf. This was the first dress Eleanor had ever worn that was not a short "little girl" dress. She had sewn new buttons, white as pearls, down the front. The brassiere from Aunt Velma was underneath. Eleanor felt very grown-up.

She helped Lila with the buttons on the back of her dress, a white ankle-length muslin with a high collar, a blousy bodice and sleeves, and a wide sash at the waist. Lila wore her hair up the same way their mother wore hers in Eleanor's tea-tin picture. She pinched her cheeks and lips to give them color.

They had only a small hand mirror that had been their mother's, and Lila could not see all of herself at once. "You are truly a glowing bride," Eleanor assured her. People did not often call Lila pretty, but today she was.

Together, the whole family walked past the fish shack and Mr. Fulcher's store down to the Church of Two Hundred Trees. Papa was so handsome! His handlebar mustache was carefully waxed, and his dark hair slicked back. He wore his old black suit, and the sleeves of the topcoat were only a little short. Lila had spent nearly twenty minutes with the flatirons muscling starch into his shirt. Papa's sun-browned hands and broad face seemed even darker in contrast to the whiteness of his stiff shirt.

Frank strolled down the road in his store-bought suit, straw hat, and bow tie, looking every bit like "the prettiest boy in Atlantic Grove," as Virgie Mae called him. Eleanor wished someone could take a photograph of Papa and Frank walking side by side in their finery, Papa handsome in his rough way and Frank in his dapper way, looking like father and son in spite of themselves. They were both on their best behavior, and someone looking at the photograph years later would never know they didn't get along.

Iona picked up the skirt of Lila's dress so it wouldn't get dusty. Lila complained that everyone could see her knees, but Iona ignored her and walked beside her carrying the skirt while hollering at Jesse Junior and Clarence not to climb the scrub pines and get sap on their good dungarees.

Reverend Willis only came every third Sunday to preach in Atlantic Grove, and Lila had planned the wedding for one of his days. The wedding guests sat in semicircles on wooden benches. Iona and Eleanor had collected red, pink, and yellow roses and startling white gardenias from their gardens and put them in a vase by the window, and their strong sweet aroma filled the room. They had selected the prettiest and fullest blooms for Lila's bouquet.

There was no piano or organ in the church, so Uncle Owen began to play Enrico Caruso on the Victrola when Lila and Papa came in, but Reverend Willis asked him to stop because he said the music was irreverent. Eleanor missed the music, but the sounds of the water and wind outside quickly filled the silence. Papa linked his big arm through Lila's and watched his feet carefully as they walked down the aisle so as not to step on any bench legs. He looked as if his shirt made his neck itch.

Eleanor sat between Iona and Aunt Velma in the front row. Iona, with her shoulders erect, folded her big worn hands over her rounded stomach and did not smile during the whole service. She wore a new cotton print dress, and her thin brown hair was knotted in a clean, shiny bun at the nape of her neck. Jesse Junior and Clarence, next to her, swung their feet back and forth until she smacked their knees. Aunt Velma, gripping Eleanor's hand, dabbed at the corners of her eyes with Uncle Owen's handkerchief. Eleanor looked out the window and saw a column of sunshine slide from behind a cloud and highlight the white headstones in the cemetery across the road. She counted three headstones over in the fourth row, where her mother was buried. Mama would be happy for Lila today.

Caleb's brand-new black suit fairly hung on him. His hair was parted and combed flat, and his Adam's apple danced up and down above his bow tie. He wiped his brow again and again while Lila patted his calloused hand.

When the Methodist minister leaned forward, his

Bible open in his hands, and asked if Lila took Caleb to be her lawfully wedded husband, Eleanor heard no hesitation in Lila's firm voice as she said, "I do." Her doubts from the night before seemed to be gone. Everyone stood and applauded and there was a chorus of "Amen!" when Caleb, quick as lightning, pecked Lila on the cheek, his long, thin neck like a bird's.

Eleanor thought something momentous ought to occur. After all, Lila's life, Caleb's, and her own, were changed forever now. But nothing momentous happened at all. The cedars kept swaying outside the window, light continued to slant through the church windows in exactly the same way, and everyone kept smiling and fanning themselves, elbow to elbow in the small sanctuary.

Eleanor stepped forward, threw her arms around Lila, and began to cry. Lila gently peeled her off and held her at arm's length, framing her face with her warm and steady hands.

"Hush up, now, sister, hush up." She wiped Eleanor's cheeks with her thumbs. Eleanor sniffled and nodded, embarrassed at showing such emotion with all this family present.

Then Frank came and wrapped his arms around them both. "Mrs. Varnam, I presume," he said, kissing Lila's hand.

Eleanor looked for Papa then, thinking he would congratulate the newly married couple, but Papa, who hated social occasions of any kind and wasn't much of a church-goer, was already standing outside the front door with his back to everyone, facing the cemetery.

Afterward they all walked down the road to the house. Iona's boys ran alongside and got their good dungarees wet in the sound. Eleanor wondered why Iona did not scold them, but then realized Iona was not there. She looked back and saw her at the cemetery, standing beside their mother's tombstone with her head bowed. Eleanor left the others and went back to stand beside her.

"I wish Mama could have been here today," Iona said gruffly after they stood in silence for a minute or so.

"Tell me what she was like," said Eleanor.

Iona tilted her head, as if remembering. "She liked weddings. She liked pretty things. She liked books and music and romance. There's nothing romantic about being a fisherman's wife."

"You're a fisherman's wife, and now so is Lila."

Iona nodded. "Come on, let's go serve up cake and pie."

Uncle Owen hauled his Victrola back to the house and put on his Caruso recording again, and Reverend Willis, who had come along, did not complain this time. Aunt Velma opened the bottles of Pepsi-Cola and served a little to each of the adults, and Eleanor and Iona sliced up the cake and pies. Clarence and Jesse Junior were pleased as punch to get their own chunks of shaved ice.

Frank parked himself in Papa's rocking chair, with his flat-brimmed straw hat resting on his knee, and told stories about Washington, Mexico, and the Panama Canal to Gertrude and any of the other guests who would listen. He embarrassed Eleanor by telling about her driving lesson, including the details about Miss Speckle and the wild ride down the beach. Everyone laughed, and Gertrude said, "Oh, Frank, you must teach me to drive, too!" Eleanor noticed that Gertrude, in a tight skirt short enough to show her ankles, brought Frank a glass of Pepsi-Cola and two slices of pie.

The ice rattled in the glass in Papa's big hands. He put the glass on the sink and pulled at his tie as he went out on the porch. Now that the wedding was over, Papa was ready for everyone to go home.

The bride and groom walked across the yard arm in arm, Caleb skinny and bow-legged and Lila solid beside him, and everyone followed. On the front porch of the house Caleb and Papa had built, Caleb hoisted Lila into his arms. Everyone clapped, partly because Caleb was not a big man and lifting Lila was no easy feat. Then he carried her across the threshold and, with a shove of his foot, shut the door behind him.

Eleanor stared at the closed house, with Lila and Caleb inside and her outside. Frank came over and put his arm around her. "You'll miss her."

"She'll only be next-door," she said. Now who would listen to her complain about Papa, or hear about every little thing that happened at school, or scratch her back at night?

"Fraa-nk!" called Gertrude in a singsong voice from the front seat of the Model T. "Are you coming?"

"Be right there," Frank called back, waving his hat. "We're going for a ride," he said to Eleanor. "Like to come along?"

Gertrude knitted her brow briefly in Eleanor's direction. "That's all right," Eleanor said.

Frank crossed the yard and executed a one-armed vault over the car door into the driver's seat. "Frank, you daredevil, you!" Gertrude cried.

Eleanor went back to the house and helped Iona and Aunt Velma shake out the tablecloth and wash dishes. As she collected empty cups and saucers, she replayed in her mind exactly who sat where, what they had to eat or drink, and what they said. It would be a long time before she experienced such an event again.

"You'll miss your sister, won't you, honey?" said Aunt Velma as they finished drying the cups and plates. Iona had gone home to feed the chickens.

"Oh, she'll be right next-door. I'll be able to visit every day." The dishes clattered as Eleanor shoved them into the cabinet.

"Of course she will, honey," said Aunt Velma. "And if you should ever want to come stay with me, you come on, now, any old time, you hear? You would get a chance to meet yourself some real beaus, not just fishermen."

"Beaus?"

"Of course! Every girl needs beaus. The more the better."

"Well, thank you, Aunt Velma, but I believe when I leave Atlantic Grove I will be going to California."

Aunt Velma's eyes widened. "California! You don't say!"

"Yes'm. With Frank."

"I see." Aunt Velma wrapped the last of her cups and saucers in cloths and put them back in the box she'd brought them in. "And have you asked your papa about it?"

Eleanor looked at the floor. "No'm."

"Um-hmm." Aunt Velma folded the dishtowel and laid it across the sink. "Well, we'll see, won't we? Meantime, you're so pretty, you'll attract beaus like bees to honey. Of course, you need to compliment them and make them feel special, the way I do Uncle Owen."

Aunt Velma was always beaming at Uncle Owen and saying, "Well, I declare, aren't you smart!" Eleanor had never thought Uncle Owen was particularly smart, since he said the same old sayings over and over, and she'd always wondered why Aunt Velma told him he was smart so very often. But now she knew. Part of her liked these glimpses into the world of grownups, while part of her wondered why things were so complicated.

"Where's Frank?" Papa, dressed in his work clothes, came into the kitchen.

"He's gone for a ride with Gertrude," said Aunt Velma.

"Well, best round them up so I can take you all home," Papa said.

"Goodness gracious, John! I'd thought to stay at least until tomorrow. Wouldn't you like me to stay, Eleanor?"

Eleanor glanced from Aunt Velma to Papa, but before she could answer, Papa said, "I'd like to be on the water within the hour so I can get back before dark." He shifted his weight from one foot to the other.

Eleanor knew better than to protest and so did Aunt Velma. While Aunt Velma packed and said quick good-byes, Eleanor ran after Frank and Gertrude and found them driving down the beach, Gertrude's hair ribbon rippling in the breeze. Uncle Owen put his Victrola under his arm, and Eleanor walked down to the fish shack to see them off. Frank suddenly decided to escort Gertrude back to New Bern and went along. Eleanor stood alone on the dock and waved as *Annis H*'s mainsail caught the wind and her prow cut the water, carrying Frank, Papa, Aunt Velma, Uncle Owen, and Gertrude farther and farther away.

Eleanor walked back toward the empty house. Lila's front door was still closed. She did not want to think about what they were doing in there. Across the road, Iona's front door was closed, too. She sat down on the porch, still in her blue flowered dress, and watched the shadow of a small cloud scoot across the lazy sparkling waters of the sound. A sea gull wheeled by with a plaintive cry.

She never thought Lila's wedding day would be the loneliest day of her life.

~ Another ~
Good-Bye

Two days later Eleanor was working in the garden, feeling very low, missing Lila, and listening to Frank's intermittent hammer strokes on the roof as he repaired some shingles, when she saw Virgie Mae coming down the path carrying an egg basket.

"Virgie Mae!" Eleanor wiped the dirt from her hands and ran down the row of sweet potatoes to meet her.

"I wanted to find out all about Lila's wedding." Virgie Mae caught her breath. "So I told Mama I had to come borrow some eggs. Our white hen laid two this morning, and I broke them both behind the shed, just so Mama'd let me come." She opened her brown eyes wide as she related the lie she'd told.

"Virgie Mae Salter, I can't believe you broke two perfectly good eggs just to see me! Let's go get us a cup of milk from Molly."

"Frank still here?" Virgie Mae whispered as they walked elbow to elbow through the yard.

"He's yonder on the other side of the roof. Papa's making him fix shingles." Eleanor called out, "Frank, say hello to Virgie Mae!"

"Ellie, I'm going to kill you!" Virgie Mae hissed, but she quickly smoothed her braids and pinched her cheeks. "Law, I bet I look a sight."

Frank's head and bare chest appeared above the eave of the roof, and he waved the hammer at Virgie Mae.

"Hello, Virgie Mae. How are you?"

"I'm doing just fine, thank you kindly," said Virgie Mae sweetly. To Eleanor she whispered, "He's not wearing his shirt!"

"Come down for a spell," Eleanor called. "And put your shirt back on."

"Eleanor!" Virgie Mae turned scarlet and smoothed her skirt. "You're embarrassing me."

"I'll be ready for a break soon," Frank called, then the hammering resumed.

"He may be just a big brother to you," said Virgie Mae, "but to me he's the most fascinating man who ever lived in these parts." Eleanor remembered Gertrude flirting with Frank at the wedding. She ought to tell Virgie Mae the truth to keep her from acting foolish.

Eleanor took two tin cups to the live oak where Molly liked to graze. Lila didn't like her snitching milk from Molly in the middle of the day, but Virgie Mae was company, wasn't she? She leaned her head up against Molly's warm side, inhaling her thick cow smell, and squeezed a pink teat until both cups were full of warm foaming milk. Then she and Virgie Mae went to sit on the porch.

"Well, was Lila's wedding just grand?" Virgie Mae's freckled face looked so eager for every detail, Eleanor could almost see the pictures forming behind her eyes as she described Lila's dress, the flowers, the Victrola, the Pepsi-Cola, the pies, and the brassieres. She told her everything except about Frank and Gertrude.

"I'll have to show you the brassiere," Eleanor said and ran inside to fetch it, still talking. She left Virgie Mae sitting on the porch, her knees to her chin, with her skirt pulled down over her legs like a tent and her bare feet crossed at the ankles. Then Eleanor heard Frank's voice. Craning her neck slightly to see through the doorway, Eleanor could see that Frank was standing with one foot on the porch step. His dark, wavy hair was damp with sweat at the hairline. He'd had the good manners to put on his shirt. Eleanor watched Virgie Mae duck her head and blush the color of an unripe blackberry.

Eleanor put the brassiere away and stopped talking, since Virgie Mae wasn't listening anyway. She couldn't catch what they were saying to each other because their conversation was in low tones, but she heard Virgie Mae's frequent giggles. She noticed how Frank inclined his head toward Virgie Mae, who reminded Eleanor of a little bird, ducking and fluffing and fidgeting.

"Eleanor," Frank said when she rejoined them, "how about a ride in the Model T? Virgie Mae's agreed to go."

"But what about the shingles?" Eleanor heard herself ask. "You promised Papa you'd finish today."

"It won't take more than fifteen minutes to drive from one end of Atlantic Grove to the other," said Frank. "That leaves plenty of time to finish the roof."

Eleanor started to protest but saw how excited Virgie Mae looked and remembered how badly she herself had wanted a ride. She sat down next to Virgie Mae and took a sip of milk. "Will your mama have a fit?" she asked Virgie Mae.

Frank grinned. "What Virgie Mae's mama doesn't know won't hurt her."

"Frank says he'll let me try driving, just like you did!" said Virgie Mae.

"Well, what are we waiting for?" Frank threw the hammer on the ground and took Virgie Mae's hand to help her down from the porch. Delighted, Virgie Mae put down her cup of milk and followed Frank across the yard. Eleanor climbed into the backseat so Virgie Mae could sit in front. Frank pushed up the spark, opened the throttle, and pulled back the hand lever. On the third crank the engine caught, and the car bounced across the yard.

The roads in Atlantic Grove were narrow and rutted, but the sky was blue as a baby's eyes, and there was a slight breeze, unusual for June. People working in their gardens or yards waved as the Model T chugged by. Frank made a point of not passing Virgie Mae's house.

Eleanor wondered if Virgie Mae didn't scream with excitement a little too much. She looked at Frank adoringly, while Eleanor was pretty sure her brother was just passing time to get a break from working on the shingles.

Frank took the car down to the beach so Virgie Mae would have plenty of open space for learning, but she didn't take to driving the way Eleanor had. She had a hard time coordinating the clutch and the hand lever.

"Oh, I give up!" she finally said, after three or four false starts. "I feel like I'm going to shake the teeth out of our heads!" She put her hands in her lap, smiling brightly at Frank. "I guess automobile driving is for men."

"Try again!" Eleanor cried. "Don't give up. It's like casting a fishnet, or knitting, or writing your letters—it's easy once you get the hang of it."

"No, really, I'm happy just to ride along." Virgie Mae got out of the driver's seat and ran around the car to the passenger side. "I like it when Frank drives."

Eleanor frowned. Virgie Mae would never learn if she gave up so easily. "Well, if you're sure you don't want to, I'll drive," Eleanor heard herself say.

"Sure, Miss Priss, take us for a spin!" Frank threw his legs over the front seat and slid into the back. Eleanor scrambled from backseat to front, and Virgie Mae, not looking pleased, got in the passenger seat beside her.

"Just because I can't do it, you don't have to show off," Virgie Mae grumbled as she slammed the door.

"I'm not showing off. I think you gave up too easily."

Virgie Mae turned her face away. "Virgie Mae!" Eleanor said, but her friend wouldn't look at her, so finally Eleanor got out and cranked the car and drove home. She started trying to explain to Virgie Mae how to press the clutch pedal down in a smooth motion, but Virgie Mae pointedly turned away with her arms crossed over her chest, so Eleanor stopped talking. By the time she pulled the Model T back into the yard, she had lost herself in the fun of driving and had almost forgotten about Virgie Mae being angry.

"Ellie, you are as fine a driver as any man I know," Frank said as he climbed out of the back. Eleanor smiled, but then glanced at Virgie Mae's pinched lips and felt miserable.

"Well," said Frank, "that was right much fun. I'll just get the sand off her." He sauntered over to the well to pump a bucket of water. Virgie Mae's yearning eyes followed him. Then, without a word to Eleanor, she marched across the yard to get her egg basket.

"Virgie Mae, it just takes time. It took me a few tries before I could do it."

"Do you have any eggs to spare or not?" asked Virgie Mae tartly.

"Why, of course, I have plenty," said Eleanor. "And we still need to finish our milk."

"I'd best be getting home." Virgie Mae stayed in the yard.

Eleanor found two eggs and placed them gently in Virgie Mae's basket. "Sit a minute with me and finish our milk."

"I'd better not."

"I didn't mean to make you mad."

"Oh, now Frank thinks you're more clever than I am!"

Eleanor wanted to say that she felt sure Frank barely thought about Virgie Mae at all. This was the time to tell her about Gertrude, but somehow she just couldn't say the words. "You shouldn't think about him," she said instead.

"How can you say that? You know I've admired him practically forever!"

"Because he doesn't think of us, Virgie Mae, or this place. He thinks of California. This past week he's gotten two letters from fellows he met while he was working in Panama, asking him to join them in San Francisco."

"San Francisco?"

"He read the letters out loud to us at the dinner table. His friends wrote him about endless sunshine, about fruits and vegetables as big as flour barrels, about new businesses springing up like weeds, and about new millionaires being born every day." Eleanor realized that she was not just trying to convince Virgie Mae to stop thinking about Frank, but herself as well. She saw the hurt in her friend's face. "I'm sorry I showed off." She touched Virgie Mae's bony shoulder.

"It's all right. I'm sorry I acted like a pill."

"You ought to break eggs more often." Eleanor grinned.

"I'd best go, really." Virgie Mae squeezed Eleanor's hand. "Mama will wonder where I've got to."

"I'll go with you partway."

They went together between the neat rows in the garden, then Eleanor watched Virgie Mae walk down the road until she was indistinguishable from the shimmering sea oats. She missed Lila. Even when her sister was grumpy it was better than being alone. She looked out into the yard and saw Frank still tinkering with his automobile instead of working on the shingles. Fear swept over her. Could Papa have seen them again from the sound?

That night when Papa came home, Frank still had not finished repairing the roof. Eleanor was baking some sweet potatoes and getting the pan ready for whatever fish Papa brought home. "Well, Eleanor," he said, as he handed her the pail with two small spot to cook. "I reckon now Lila's married, you're the woman of the house."

Being the woman of the house meant cooking and cleaning and washing and mending clothes and caring for the garden. And it had not taken long to occur to Eleanor that if she was doing all that she would be hard-pressed to find time for school. Dorcas Webster had stopped going to school just last year to keep house for her father and brothers and younger sisters. Eleanor chopped the heads off the spot and slapped them into the pan, where they began to sizzle.

"Shingles done, Frank?" Papa asked.

"Almost." Frank was sitting in Papa's rocking chair with the two letters he'd received about California open on his lap.

"Thought you said you'd finish today."

"Well, it's taking longer than I thought." Frank folded the letters and put them in his pocket.

"Any carpenter worth his salt would be finished by now. I'd like to know what you've been doing. I don't take kindly to the idea of a person living under my roof and not earning his keep."

"I'm earning my keep!" Frank sat up sharply. "You'd best not accuse me of living off your charity!"

"You've never been a decent worker." Papa paced the room. "You've always been a lazy, good-for-nothing dreamer with highfalutin ideas that never did nobody any good."

"Papa, why don't you sit down and eat," Eleanor said quickly, serving up a plate. "You'll feel better." She remembered Iona and Lila saying this, so she said it, too. Had he seen them in the car?

"I'm not hungry!" Papa shouted at Eleanor, then turned to Frank. "And get out of my chair!"

Frank stood up. His face was white. "Many a man would be proud of a son who earned enough to buy an automobile like that," he said.

"Can't eat an automobile, can we?" Papa shot back, his voice rising. "You think I don't know you've been playing cards and drinking whiskey down at the recreation hall. That is the road to ruination, and you know it, Frank Hill."

Eleanor stood stock still at the sink, holding Papa's plate. Playing cards? Drinking whiskey?

"It is no sin to play a hand of cards for enjoyment. Nor is it a sin to enjoy a glass of whiskey in moderation," said Frank.

"They're sins in my book, and that makes them sins in my house!"

"You won't be bothered with me in your house any longer, sir!" Frank stalked out, letting the screen door slam behind him. Papa sat down and stayed stone silent for several long minutes. Eleanor put his plate before him, but he ignored it. A few minutes later he got up from the table and left the house. Eleanor stood by herself at the sink.

So that was why Papa was mad. She had visions of Frank sitting in a smoky room playing cards with evil-looking men and drinking whiskey. She had been taught by Papa and at church that these activities *were* sins, and she was sad that her own brother would do such things.

Papa came back inside after a spell and ate his cold supper without speaking to Eleanor. By bedtime Frank still had not returned.

The next morning Eleanor woke from a restless sleep thinking someone was standing over her. When she opened her eyes, she saw Frank holding his duffel bag. He knelt beside her bed. His breath had that same sweet smell as the night he sat in his car drinking from the tall bottle.

"I'm leaving, Miss Priss."

"No!"

"I have to, Ellie."

"Take me with you!" She tangled her feet in the bed-clothes in her hurry to get out of bed and looked down from her loft toward Papa's room. The door was open, which meant Papa had left on *Annis H* already. "I can be ready in a jiffy. I can help you. I can cook, I can wash your shirts, I can drive!"

"Stop right there, Miss Priss. You're not going any-where." Frank put his hands on her shoulders. "Now, it just won't do for me to drag a twelve-year-old sister across the country."

"I'm *thirteen* now."

"I may have done some crazy things in my life, but nothing *that* crazy. You'd best stay here."

Eleanor thought she would sink right into the floor. Frank's face seemed to shrink, and his lips moved as if he were talking from a long way away.

"I'll write and tell you all about San Francisco. And when I become a millionaire I'll send train fare for all of you, and we'll live in a fancy house on top of Nob Hill."

"Frank! I want to go now, you can't just leave me here!" It didn't matter if she cried or not because there was no one else in the house to hear. She wrapped her arms around his waist and buried her head in his shirt and cried until there wasn't one drop left to come out.

Frank held her without saying a thing. He patted her back and hugged her close. When she stopped, he pushed her away gently. "I've got to go. The mailboat leaves in twenty minutes."

"I'm at least coming to the dock with you."

They cranked the Model T and drove in silence down to the dock as the edge of the sun slid up over the water. Some of the fishermen helped Frank get the Model T onto a flat-bottom skiff. The mirrorlike hood glinted in the early morning light.

"I hope all those trees and waves and mountains are big enough for you out there," Eleanor said, her puffy lips brushing Frank's cheek.

"Good-bye, Miss Priss. Tell Papa he got his wish. I'm gone." He looked away for a minute, then leaped onto the skiff with his duffel bag.

Hot, salty tears seeped into the edges of Eleanor's mouth. She waded in ankle-deep and helped shove the skiff into the water. It drifted out several feet, and then as the mailboat edged away from the dock, Frank tossed a rope to the skipper. The mailboat chugged away, pulling Frank and his Model T behind it. Frank smiled and raised one hand in farewell. Eleanor watched his figure shrink as the skiff slid across the gray-brown sound, leaving her and Atlantic Grove behind.

PART TWO

New Bern

~ *Lila's Baby* ~

Eleanor chopped potatoes for clam chowder at Lila's sink. Lila and Caleb's house, like Papa's, was made of split wooden rails and had a floor raised about three feet from the ground to protect against high water. There was one room for eating, one for sleeping, and a small loft up above. The house was held together in key places with machine-made nails that Papa had traded scallops for, but the corners were held only by notches in the wood. A year had passed since Lila's wedding, but the wood in her house was still a creamy yellow and smelled sappy and fresh. Papa's house had long ago weathered gray, and it creaked in the wind and smelled musty, especially after a rain.

Eleanor was staying with Lila because her baby was due any day now and Caleb had gone on a fishing trip up the Neuse River. Lila had been feeling poorly all day and was resting in the bedroom. Iona could not help because Jesse Junior, Clarence, and her new baby girl, Callie, all had the chickenpox.

The last year had been miserable for Eleanor. Her new schoolteacher, Miss Bullard, was old and strict. She had put Eleanor in charge of teaching the first and second graders. Eleanor herself had learned nothing new at all, except how to keep five children occupied. She almost felt sick when she reread Miss Rosalie's letters and compared her dreary life to that of her former teacher.

September 25, 1913

Dear Eleanor,

Before the start of school this year, I traveled with a woman I know to Arizona to view the Grand Canyon. One cannot use words to describe the sheer majesty of that place—it is truly one of the wonders of the world. Would you believe that I descended the very steep and narrow path down the side of the canyon on the back of a mule? One woman dropped her hat, and we watched it sail two thousand feet to the bottom.

I hope you are reading the New Bern Tribune on a regular basis and keeping up with politics because women should be well-informed on political issues. Our President Woodrow Wilson is a scholar who was once president of Princeton University, and I believe he will help bring about many reforms in this country, including our system of education. He has three fine daughters who have been well-educated. Therefore I know he believes in education for women.

I have enclosed a list of books I recommend for you to read, if you can get to a library and find them. Remember that inner beauty is more precious than outward charms.

Your teacher,

Rosalie Adams

Eleanor wrote Miss Rosalie regularly. She also tried to compose entertaining letters to Frank. Sometimes she read over what she had written about school, what they had for dinner, who was sick, or what Reverend Willis said in his sermon at church, and felt desperate that she didn't have something more interesting to tell. Was it possible for anyone's life to be more boring than hers?

Over the past year they'd had only two postcards and one letter from Frank. The letter included a picture of him standing beside a line of Model Ts and pointing up to a fancy sign that read "Hill's Motor Company."

"With a partner, I have started a business buying, storing, and selling automobiles," he had written. "Soon we will be the largest automobile dealer in all of San Francisco! It is the wave of the future, and I am riding the crest!"

In the picture, Frank's shoes and jacket were new, so Eleanor knew things were going well for him. But a whole year had passed, and he had not sent train fare.

Would she ever get away from here? Somehow she had to. She had not forgotten what Aunt Velma had said about coming to live in New Bern to help her with sewing. So, she'd written her a secret letter.

May 15, 1914

Dear Aunt Velma,

How are you? How are your eyes and fingers? If you should still be in need of help with your sewing, I am a quick study and a hard worker. I would be pleased as punch to help out. Papa is out fishing most days and can do without me, and I believe Lila will soon be able to spare me, too, after the baby comes. How far away is the high school?

Your niece,
Eleanor Hill

Yesterday when she checked for mail she saw Papa had gotten a letter from Aunt Velma. What did it say? On the way home she pressed her fingers against the envelope, trying to read what was written inside, but she couldn't make out the words.

"Look, Papa, a letter from Aunt Velma," she said when she took it to him. "Wonder what she has to say." But Papa grunted without interest and did not open it. Later when she took his supper over, she saw to her great frustration that the letter was still lying unopened on the table.

This morning after Papa took *Annis H* out, Eleanor made an excuse to Lila and ran next-door. He had finally opened it! She slid the sheet of creamy stationery from the envelope.

June 5, 1914
Dear Brother-in-Law,

It is time you gave some thought to Eleanor's future. She is fourteen now and quite a Young Lady. As she has completed the studies the Atlantic Grove Academy has to offer, and has no Marriage Prospects at this point in time, Owen and I would like to propose that she come live with us. She can help me with the sewing I take in, and if she has time, she may attend New Bern Graded School. In exchange for the sewing work we will give her room and board as well as money for tuition and books, and meanwhile perhaps she will meet an Eligible Young Man who will gladly take her on as his own responsibility.

Eleanor seems to be a hard worker and has an Agreeable Disposition and would not disrupt our household.

Sincerely,
Velma Winstead

New Bern! High school! Eleanor had stood frozen by the table for several minutes. A wave of goose bumps started at her fingers and rushed right up to the tips of her ears. This was it—the day her tedious life changed forever.

She ran to show the letter to Lila. Lying back on her bed, Lila propped the letter on her belly to read it. Afterward she frowned and said nothing but "Papa would never allow it."

Eleanor protested, but deep down she knew Lila was right. How could she talk him into it? Today she'd done her chores in a foggy, dreamlike state. Nothing mattered except somehow being able to go.

"Ellie!" Lila called from the bedroom. Eleanor pushed the door open, wiping her hands on the dishtowel. Lila sat hunched on the edge of the bed, her hands moving in circles over her rounded stomach.

"Go get Mrs. Taylor." Lila looked to be in terrible pain. Eleanor's heart thudded against her ribs, and her head was a jumble of panic. "Tell her it's time," Lila groaned, and lay back on the bed as if she couldn't find a position that was comfortable. "Hurry."

Eleanor shut the door and took a deep breath, trying to calm herself. The Taylors' house was almost half a mile away. She took the clam chowder off the stove to stop it cooking and stood uncertainly with it, trying to decide what to do. At last she put the whole steaming pot on the table and started off down the road at a run.

What if something terrible happened to Lila? How unfair for Iona's children to have the chickenpox right when the baby was being born.

She slowed to a walk. Just past a stand of cedars ahead she could see the roofline of the Taylors' cottage.

Almost there. She could hear nothing but her own breath roaring in her ears as she approached the house. Rocking chairs with peeling paint lined the wide porch. A rope swing hung on one of the lower branches of a live oak in the yard, and Nat Taylor sat on it, steering his feet in a circular path around a muddy hole beneath him. Although he had dropped out of school to fish with his father, Papa said Nat was lazy and many days did not go out on the boat.

Nat looked up and squinted at Eleanor. He was tanned and muscular from fishing, but had the same bruised-looking eyes and floppy black hair as always. Eleanor could tell Mrs. Taylor simply put a bowl on his head and cut around it.

"It's the suffragette," Nat said sourly.

"I need to talk to your mama." Eleanor held her chin high and marched across the sandy yard.

"She ain't here."

"What?" Eleanor crossed the porch, still gasping for

breath. "Mrs. Taylor!" she called as she knocked on the front door, which was slightly ajar. "Help, Lila needs you!"

"Told you she ain't here. Gone to Sealevel to deliver a baby." Nat's narrow eyes cut at her.

A pain stabbed Eleanor's chest and she felt lightheaded. What should she do? "Nat, you must tell her the minute she gets here to come to Lila. Please." She ran back toward home in a fever. As she ran by Virgie Mae's house she spotted her not far from the road collecting chicken eggs.

"Eleanor!" Virgie Mae called. "Is Lila's time come?"

"Yes, and Mrs. Taylor's gone to Sealevel. Is your mama home?"

"No, her pappy's sick, and she's gone to take care of him. But I helped with cousin Lucy's baby last month. I'll come with you!" Virgie Mae dropped the egg basket on the ground and ducked through the yaupon bushes, and they both pounded down the road at a dead run. "Mama will die, I probably broke every one of those eggs," she said between breaths.

The sun was dropping behind the dunes, but the breeze that ruffled the sea oats was hot and dry. Eleanor imagined Lila, lying on her bed, holding onto her stomach, and grew more and more worried.

When they reached Lila's house there were three scrawny, wild cats on the table arrayed like the spokes of a wagon wheel around Eleanor's clam chowder, their small heads ducked out of sight below the rim of the pot.

"Oh no!" Eleanor cried. "Shoo! Shoo, now, scat!" They streaked out the door, off the porch, and into the underbrush.

Eleanor heard Lila groan in the back room, and she began to cry.

"Hush up, Eleanor, let me think," said Virgie Mae. "The first thing Mrs. Taylor did when cousin Lucy had her baby was to boil a big pot of water."

The clam chowder was already in the big pot, and Eleanor could think of nowhere else to put it, so she lugged the chowder to the side of the house and threw it out under the yaupon bushes. Then she ran to the pump, rinsed and filled the pot, hauled it in, and put it on the stove.

Virgie Mae had gone into the bedroom and shut the door. Just as Eleanor sat down at the table and swallowed a sob, Virgie Mae stuck her head out. Her face was pale, but she seemed amazingly calm. "When I holler at you that I want something, you bring it to me, you hear?"

"All right," Eleanor said. For what seemed like the next several hours she sat at the kitchen table, watching the shadows lengthen, and listening to the sounds from the bedroom. She tore strips of cloth and dropped them in the boiling water as Virgie Mae instructed. She lit the kerosene lamp when it was dark. Suddenly she heard the screen door slam and Mrs. Taylor stood there, her damp gray hair curling around her thin, lined face.

"Lord," she said in a weary voice. "The moon goes full, and these babies all get a mind to come at once." She pushed up her sleeves. "Is no one with Lila?"

"Virgie Mae." Eleanor's voice was thin and wavery.

"No time for nonsense." Mrs. Taylor briefly gripped Eleanor's shoulder with one sinewy hand. "She's a strong girl, sugar, she should be fine."

Mrs. Taylor went straight into the bedroom, but before she closed the door Eleanor saw Virgie Mae throw her arms around her, saying, "Oh, thank goodness you're here!"

Eleanor kept water boiling and handed in whatever Mrs. Taylor asked for. She fell asleep sometime during the night and woke in the gray dawn, stiff on the kitchen chair. Mrs. Taylor was outside hanging wet sheets on the line. Virgie Mae was asleep on Eleanor's pallet. She heard a cry and thought one of the wild cats had somehow gotten into the house. But it wasn't a cat. It was Lila's baby, finally come.

"Eleanor!" Lila called from the bedroom. "Bring me a rag. The baby has thrown up again."

Eleanor sighed. She knew now exactly where babies came from, and she was definitely not having any. One week after the birth of Lila's baby, word had gotten around that Virgie Mae had a natural-born skill for midwifery and Eleanor had a weak stomach. The joke around Atlantic Grove was that Lila's baby had come into the world just fine, but a whole basket of eggs and a pot of clam chowder had been sacrificed in the process.

The bedroom door squeaked as Eleanor pushed it open. A wave of heat and baby smells rushed up against her, and she held her breath as she handed Lila the rag. The baby was lying on her stomach as he nursed. Eleanor had been surprised to notice that Lila's stomach still looked large even after the baby came out.

Caleb and Lila had named the baby Caleb Junior. He was red and squalling, with a mass of spiky black hair that

Mrs. Taylor predicted would fall out, and then new hair would grow, and there was no telling what color it would be. His eyes were milky and unfocused, and Eleanor did not think he could see very well. Lila had asked Eleanor several times if she wanted to hold him, but she always said, "No, thank you." He was squirmy and smelled like sour milk.

"There's your aunt Eleanor, sugar pie. What do you say to that?" Lila regarded Eleanor briefly, then busied herself with cleaning the baby's face.

Eleanor could not stop thinking about going to live with Aunt Velma. It seemed selfish, with Lila still in bed and all, but she didn't see how she would get another chance to go to high school.

"There!" Lila exclaimed. "All clean. There's my handsome baby now." Lila actually seemed happy about the squalling red thing in her arms. She could not kiss the baby enough, planting soft smacks on his head, his cheeks, his dimpled shoulders, and his tummy. Stern no-nonsense Lila, smothering her baby with kisses. Eleanor could hardly believe it.

"Did Mama kiss us like that?" she asked.

"Oh yes, she kissed us plenty. She used to hold you up and say, 'I'm gonna eat you right up, that's how sweet you are!'" Eleanor tried to imagine what it might feel like to be that little baby and be smothered with love.

"Mama thought you were so pretty, Eleanor. She used to say over and over, 'Oh, she's the prettiest little *thing.*' And then she'd squeeze you silly."

Eleanor giggled. She wished she could remember, really

remember. She tried to picture her mother's smiling face close to her own, her eyes warm and crinkled around the edges. Her mother would have wanted her to have a wonderful, lovely life. Her mother would have wanted her to go to high school in New Bern. And right then, she made a decision. She would go without Papa's permission.

The baby pushed his mouth around on Lila's nightshirt, which still embarrassed Eleanor no matter how many times her sister told her it was the most natural thing in the world.

"Scoot on out of here. This baby needs a nap, and so do I. Take some time off for yourself, Miss Priss."

Eleanor thanked Lila and quickly ran next-door. She got her stationery from its hiding place under the bed and dashed off a letter to Aunt Velma saying that she would be coming to New Bern in just a few weeks, as soon as Lila's lying-in was past.

She raced around the yard and collected three eggs, then ran to the store. Mr. Fulcher said he would give her a stamp in exchange for the eggs if she would also dust and mop. When she handed him the letter, Papa's wrath crossed her mind briefly, but she blocked it out. Her fate was sealed.

There was no news from Frank, and walking back to Lila's, Eleanor dawdled on the beach. The sun had dropped behind the dunes, but the sand was still warm under her feet, and her shadow on the beach was long and thin. Eleanor liked to pretend she was an elegant lady when her shadow was tall and willowy at sunset.

"It's a pleasure to meet you." She curtseyed and offered an imaginary gentleman her hand to kiss. "Thank you, I'm finding New Bern perfectly delightful," she said, watching her slim graceful shadow.

The sun slid lower, and a cool breeze brushed Eleanor's arm, raising goose bumps. Her shadow melted into the dark sand. The sighs of the wind and the cries of the gulls reminded her of Lila's ordeal. She was mystified, after what she had seen Lila go through, why women would want to have babies.

If she didn't get away from Atlantic Grove, with the droning sameness of the tide coming in and going out, she would die. Papa, Lila, Iona, and Virgie Mae would have to understand. She would go to New Bern, attend high school, and become an independent woman. Miss Rosalie would be so proud.

Eleanor's New Life

Eleanor had lived fourteen years in her loft, in the house by the sound. Her trunk lay open, and everything she owned was in it—her nightgown and underthings, Mama's shoes, a hand-me-down dress from Lila, her dress from Lila's wedding (which was too small in the bust now), an apron, a sweater Iona had knitted, a wool coat, the brassiere from Aunt Velma (also outgrown), and her tea tin. Before closing the trunk, Eleanor opened the tea tin and looked again at Mama's picture. Even though her mother had her hair swept up in a grown-up style, her face looked young. She was the same age as Eleanor—fourteen—but already married.

Eleanor folded the bed quilt she and Lila had made from scraps and put it in the top of the trunk. She had slept under that quilt many nights and couldn't part with it.

Papa had never given his permission for her to go to New Bern. He had never addressed the topic at all. He'd already left on *Annis H*, and Eleanor felt guilty sneaking away just the way Frank had, so she wrote him a note, which made her feel better, but did not disguise the fact that she was going without his permission. She left it on the table.

Dear Papa,

I hope you understand that I want to go to high school in New Bern to make something better of myself, and that you will be proud of me.

Go to Iona's or Lila's for supper every night. I will write you often.

Your daughter,
Eleanor

She wanted to sign it "your loving daughter," but something kept her from it. When she finished, she put down the pen and ran to Lila's. Waves of September heat rose, shimmering, from the sand. There was no breeze. Lila came to the door with Caleb Junior in her arms.

"I'm ready!"

"Slow down, girl—we're not going to a fire," grumbled Lila.

Although it was early, Caleb had left to go fishing, and Lila had already swept up, fed the chickens, milked Molly, tended the garden, and had the wash bucket and laundry gathered for the day's washing.

Eleanor next ran across the road to Iona's, and she came to the door holding Callie in her left arm and pulling along Jesse Junior and Clarence with her right. Jesse Senior had already taken his boat out.

"I got chores waiting," said Iona. "Let's get this over with." She shifted Callie to her hip and went with Eleanor to fetch her trunk. Lila came behind with Caleb Junior and the boys. As they walked through the sandy yard, Eleanor turned and looked back at the sagging wooden cottage. Miss Speckle and the other chickens sat in the shade of the crawlspace under the porch, the sea oats bowed, and the leaves on the live oak trembled in the breeze like many hands waving good-bye.

"With you leaving, now we'll have Papa to put up with," Lila said as they followed the path toward the dock. "Thanks a lot, sister."

Eleanor glanced at her sisters. "I'm sorry. I'll write every week and tell you what high school is like."

"I'd be mighty surprised if Aunt Velma lets you out of the sewing room to go to high school," said Iona.

"Aunt Velma's no fool," said Lila. "If you think you're going to be living on easy street once you get to New Bern, you've got another thing coming."

What grumps her sisters were! They'd acted the same way about Frank leaving.

As they neared the dock, Eleanor looked for Virgie Mae. She had said she would try to come say good-bye.

Iona and Eleanor set down the trunk, and they all sat on top of it and waited for the mailboat. Eleanor thought about the letter she had received from Aunt Velma, which she had reread just that morning:

September 11, 1914
Dear Eleanor,
This summer is the hottest I can remember, and it seems

there is no relief from the humidity. Just to lift a finger wears me to a Frazzle.

I have not received any word from your father. Perhaps his letter got lost.

Uncle Owen and I will meet the mailboat at the dock the last Monday in September, as you wrote in your letter. I will look forward to the Conviviality of having a young person in the house.

You will have more Marriage Opportunities in New Bern.

Sincerely,
Aunt Velma

The silhouette of a vessel appeared on the horizon. "There's the mailboat," Iona said, standing up. Her boys climbed to the top of the pile of oyster shells to get a better view.

"Remember when Frank brought his automobile?" Eleanor said to Lila.

"I thought it was the ugliest thing I ever saw," Lila replied.

"And I thought it was beautiful." It seemed like a long time since Frank had come home with the car.

The mailboat captain, a greasy-skinned, silent man named Crabby, pulled up to the dock, ignoring the entreaties of Iona's boys to let them tie up the boat. Crabby grunted a greeting and then spit some tobacco juice into the shallow water as he walked up toward Mr. Fulcher's store with the mailbag.

Iona helped Eleanor load the trunk on board. Still holding Callie, she wrapped her free arm around Eleanor and gave a quick squeeze. "Use the sense God gave you, girl," she said.

Lila stepped up and hugged Eleanor then. "Don't forget us, now, Miss High and Mighty," she said, but when they hugged Eleanor felt warm tears on Lila's cheek.

"I'll be back for a visit in no time," Eleanor said, trying not to cry. Suddenly a small figure with blond braids shot down the path and onto the dock. Virgie Mae threw herself at Eleanor.

"I'll never forgive you for leaving me behind!" She took Eleanor by the shoulders. "Write every week, and draw pictures of the hats and dresses so I can copy the patterns, you hear?"

"Aboard!" said Crabby as he headed back down toward the dock. Eleanor quickly wiped her cheeks and jumped on. She had barely sat down on her trunk when he shoved off and started the engine.

"Bye!" Eleanor called as the shore slid away. Virgie Mae buried her face in Lila's shoulder, and Lila put her free arm around her. Iona and Lila stayed with Virgie Mae, and the three of them waved until Eleanor could no longer see them. Thinking Papa might be watching from afar, she searched the sound without success for *Annis H.* Then she gave up and swung her legs over to the other side of her trunk so she could face the direction she was going.

Crabby did not talk to her at all. The sound was calm, and the sun felt warm on Eleanor's arms and face. She had brought bread and water for lunch but was too excited to eat, and in the end tore the bread into bits and tossed it to the crying gulls. She kept her gaze fastened on the far shore, remembering her last visit to New Bern.

She had been ten years old. That summer she had gone with Lila to stay with Aunt Velma and Uncle Owen for New Bern's bicentennial celebration. Hundreds of people lined Middle Street for the parade. The floats, drawn by horses, had left Eleanor and Lila open-mouthed in astonishment. One float carried half a dozen cannons as well as Naval officers standing at attention in their striking uniforms, spanking white down to their shoes. Eleanor's favorite float was a cart pulled by two Shetland ponies and decorated with flowers to resemble a birdcage. Inside the cage was a pretty girl about Eleanor's age. The inscription on the float read "A Bird in a Gilded Cage."

After the parade they went to Aunt Velma's house. She and Uncle Owen didn't have to use an outside well for water, and they even had a bathroom inside the house! Aunt Velma showed Eleanor and Lila how to pull the handle in the water closet so the water got sucked down a hole in the bottom like magic. The sisters even got to take a bath in Aunt Velma's claw-foot bathtub, and they marveled at how the water flowed out of the faucet, clear and warm.

Eleanor and Lila walked around Aunt Velma's house, touching things, testing the couches, and rocking in the rocking chairs. Aunt Velma owned things that had no real purpose except to be beautiful—such as an ornamental glass globe with a bluish green pattern that looked like a flower inside. When the sun set, Uncle Owen punched a button on the wall, and the room flooded with soft, yellow light. The electric lights didn't smell bad or throw off black, oily smoke like the kerosene lamps Papa lit in the evenings.

As always, Uncle Owen quoted old sayings, such as "A rolling stone gathers no moss" and "Pretty is as pretty does." At the time of their visit, Frank had been gone more than a year. When Eleanor returned home, she wrote him a letter with a list of all the old sayings quoted by Uncle Owen that weekend. She enjoyed imagining him in Washington, chuckling as he read it.

Eleanor's thoughts returned to the present as Crabby spit a yellow stream of tobacco juice into the water. Her thick braids ruffled in the constant, warm breeze. New Bern was going to be such an adventure. Aunt Velma would be there to help her, but in many ways she would really and truly be on her own. She felt very grown-up. At the same time, she couldn't help but feel guilty about those she left behind, especially Lila and Virgie Mae.

The waves rocked the boat gently, and Eleanor soon felt drowsy. The mailboat made its way up the mouth of the Neuse River, where the Trent River, not much more than a creek, emptied into it. They passed the *Pamlico,* a steam-driven coast-guard cutter, which was docked in the Trent right next to the shipyard. Next they passed several boats with crow's-nests high on their masts.

"Look," said Crabby, addressing Eleanor for the first time all morning. "There's a fellow up on that crow's-nest."

Eleanor looked up and, sure enough, she could see an older boy standing on the edge of the crow's-nest of one of the boats. He must have been a hundred feet up.

"That fellow needs to have his head examined," Crabby said.

"Dive!" someone shouted, and Eleanor saw three or four more young men gesturing at him from a small home-made raft floating beside the boat.

Everyone was watching the young man in the crow's-nest. Eleanor held her breath. He stood very tall and suddenly seemed to be looking right at her. He held his arms out by his sides and then, with a whoop, dove. For a moment he seemed suspended in midair, like an enormous bird, and then his body hurtled down.

The next second he sliced into the water, and everyone on the raft cheered. He surfaced a moment later and with a strong stroke swam, not for the raft, but for the mailboat. He crossed the twenty yards between them quickly.

"You ought to be in reform school!" shouted Crabby, gunning the motor.

"I did it to show my admiration for the charming and lovely young lady," the young man shouted as he swam to keep up with the boat.

Eleanor felt her face get hot. She memorized his wet black hair and smiling face, the water streaming from his eyelashes.

Crabby scowled at him. Eleanor didn't dare speak to the young man, because she knew that was improper, but she watched him swim back and climb onto the raft with the others and listened to their hearty laughter until the raft shrank to the size of a gull on the water.

Turning to face forward, she saw the Neuse River Bridge and the dock at the foot of Middle Street. Not long after, she saw the masts of the oyster boats. At the edge of the dock, taking care not to get too close to the bushels of craggy, black-and-white oyster shells, stood Aunt Velma and Uncle Owen. Eleanor climbed across an oyster boat, and Uncle Owen helped her up onto the slick, fishy dock.

"Eleanor!" Aunt Velma hugged her tightly. "I was afraid you wouldn't leave your papa."

"Here I am," said Eleanor.

"All's well that ends well," said Uncle Owen.

Life at Aunt Velma and Uncle Owen's was a whirl. School was to begin in just one week, and Aunt Velma determined that Eleanor needed one or two nice dresses like the other girls at New Bern Graded School. She took Eleanor to the dry goods and mercantile to buy material for the dresses, as well as pencils and writing paper. Previously Eleanor had never used anything in school but a tablet. Aunt Velma said Eleanor could attend school in the morning, sew in the afternoon, and still have time in the evening for homework.

Aunt Velma used the front bedroom upstairs, where the light was best, for sewing. She charged five cents for a hem, ten cents to reverse a worn collar, and sometimes as much as three dollars to cut and sew a dress or a suit from a pattern. Eleanor had been sewing a long time, but only for her family, and not from patterns or for pay. The stitches had to be tiny and even and invisible, if possible. Aunt Velma had her pull out many a seam and redo it. Her fingers were soon pricked and sore on the tips, but she didn't mind. Each day her work improved, and the sewing was what would allow her to go to school, so she did not complain.

Uncle Owen worked for the railroad, and to Eleanor it seemed he and Aunt Velma lived a life of luxury. They had an icebox to keep food cold. They got the *New Bern Tribune* on the very day it was printed, instead of three days later the way they did in Atlantic Grove. They didn't have a garden. Instead a Negro woman named Nettie came right down the street pulling a wagon, calling, "Fresh ve-ge-tebles! Turnips, cabbage, string beans!" Aunt Velma could go to the butcher's for fresh meat and fish, and a man even brought milk right to their door.

On the first day of school, Eleanor nervously walked the three blocks to the New Bern Graded School. The entire student body assembled in the auditorium and was addressed by the principal, Mr. T. J. Cooper, who began the day by reading a Bible verse and then spent a good while telling them how they should apply that verse to their everyday lives. He even talked about the sins of drinking and gambling. Eleanor looked at her lap and tried to keep her face expressionless so as not to let on that her own brother did those things.

As she sat on the wooden auditorium chair in her new pinafore, she glanced around at the other students. There were more than one hundred! Some wore store-bought outfits, but many students wore homemade clothes like hers. Aunt Velma had bought her high-top black button shoes, and she noticed with satisfaction that many of the other girls were wearing the same style. Most girls wore their hair bobbed, with zigzag waves in the front that hugged their faces from their foreheads to their chins. Her own long braids made her look like a country girl. Before the assembly began, a girl with short, shiny dark hair had poked the girl next to her, pointed to Eleanor's hair, and giggled. Eleanor had felt her face get hot, but she looked straight ahead and pretended she hadn't seen.

The seniors sat in the front rows of the auditorium, and Eleanor surprised herself by looking for the young man she had watched dive from the crow's-nest. His brown eyes were imprinted on her memory, and she knew she would recognize him if she ever saw him again. But she didn't see him and wondered if he had finished school or dropped out.

After the assembly, Eleanor went to her first class, which was English. She would have a different teacher for each subject. Students sat alphabetically according to their last name, and she felt fortunate to have a seat fairly close to the front. She took careful notes with a shaking hand as the teacher, Miss Smallwood, assigned a long poem for the students to memorize entitled *Thanatopsis*.

Eleanor found the poem in her book and panicked when she saw it was two pages long. She didn't even know the meaning of the title! Miss Smallwood told the class that the poet, William Cullen Bryant, had written the poem when he was only sixteen years old. Perhaps she meant to put them at ease with that piece of information, but somehow it made Eleanor feel even more hopeless.

After English she had Algebra, Latin, and Citizenship. She was assigned textbook chapters to study for English, problems to solve in Algebra, and sentences to write in

Latin. She was supposed to write an essay on citizenship by Friday, due the same day as the recital of *Thanatopsis*. What was worse, on Tuesday she had three more classes— Biology, Home Economics, and History.

At lunchtime she walked by herself back to Aunt Velma's house, her heart pounding in her chest. Ahead of her the New Bern girls strolled three and four abreast down the sidewalk, giggling and stopping to look in store windows.

"Sit down, dearie, I'm making egg salad for lunch," said Aunt Velma as Eleanor came into the kitchen.

Eleanor did not sit down. "I believe I'd best go back to Atlantic Grove."

"Whatever for?" Aunt Velma looked up from her mixing bowl, her fork in midair. Crumbled pale yellow egg bits clung to it.

"I'm not smart enough," Eleanor said, feeling her throat tightening.

"I never heard such foolishness!" cried Aunt Velma. "You are as smart as a whip."

"Aunt Velma, I have to memorize a poem and I don't even understand the title. I have to read chapters for English, write sentences in Latin, and solve problems in Algebra. I even have to write an essay on citizenship." She sat down heavily. "And my hair is old-fashioned. The girls made fun of me."

Aunt Velma put down her fork. She wiped her hands on the dishcloth and came over and hugged Eleanor's shoulders. Her flesh was soft and loose. Eleanor wasn't hugged very often, and she swallowed hard to keep from crying.

"I can't help you with your studies because I never graduated high school. You'll have to do that on your own. But I have always had a flair for cutting hair. I can cut yours this afternoon if you like." Aunt Velma patted Eleanor's cheek and spooned some egg salad onto a plate. "Now, eat up, child."

Eleanor ate a few bites. She drank some of Aunt Velma's sweet iced tea to wash it down and began to feel better. After some rice pudding for dessert, she began to think memorizing the poem might be possible after all.

When they'd finished lunch, Aunt Velma sat Eleanor on a stool on the back porch and pinned a towel around her shoulders. *Thanatopsis* lay open on Eleanor's lap. She read the poem to herself as Aunt Velma brushed her hair, counting to one hundred strokes. Then she read the first few lines of the poem out loud:

To him who in the love of Nature holds
Communion with her visible forms, she speaks
A various language; for his gayer hours
She has a voice of gladness, and a smile.

"Mercy, what on earth does he mean by that?" Aunt Velma wondered.

"I'm sure I haven't the foggiest," Eleanor said, repeating an expression she had heard one of the girls at school use that morning. She read farther down.

... When thoughts
Of the last bitter hour come like a blight
Over thy spirit, and sad images

Of the stern agony, and shroud, and pall,
And breathless darkness, and the narrow house,
Make thee to shudder, and grow sick at heart;—

"That is just plain morbid. Imagine a young man only sixteen thinking about such things," said Aunt Velma. "Now hold your head right still." And Eleanor heard the metallic *snip! snip!* of the scissors next to her ear. Her hair made a grassy, slithering sound as it fell. Out of the corner of her eye she saw a thick strand of it curled like a brown snake on the porch floorboards. She remembered crying over Miss Rosalie's haircut. She set her jaw and closed her eyes and turned back to *Thanatopsis.*

"You're lucky, you've got lots of natural curl," said Aunt Velma, as she continued to snip. At last she handed Eleanor a mirror. "All right, what do you think?"

Eleanor was startled to see that she had a long, elegant neck. And with a jolt she realized that she looked more grown-up than her own mother did in her treasured picture.

"Well," said Aunt Velma. "Now you're ready to meet yourself some beaus. How about that?"

Eleanor smiled obediently. If Aunt Velma wanted to think that's why she came to New Bern, let her think that. She'd pretend to be interested in young men, but all the while she'd be learning to be an independent woman like Miss Rosalie.

Ray Hamilton's Party

It wasn't long before Eleanor learned how to set her newly cut hair with curling rags so it fell in waves to her chin just like the other girls. She surprised herself by learning *Thanatopsis* one line at a time and managed to recite the whole poem in front of the English class at the end of the first week.

Her new life fell into a routine. She rose early, helped Aunt Velma get breakfast, and then walked to school. After school she returned home to help with the sewing, housework, and dinner. Sometimes in the evenings after her studies were done, she listened to musical programs on the new crystal set Uncle Owen had bought from the Sears Catalog. When he was feeling particularly fine he would crank up the Victrola. Now he had new cylinders besides the one of Enrico Caruso.

It was a luxury to have electricity because at night Eleanor was able to write to Lila, Frank, Virgie Mae, and Miss Rosalie from the green desk in her room. She'd never gotten a letter from Papa, but wrote him anyway. Lila had written that the night Eleanor left she carried Papa's dinner over and he threw it out in the yard, shouting, "Tell Eleanor since she up and left she may as well never come back!" Eleanor felt guilty about abandoning Papa and for leaving Iona and Lila with so much work. She was leading an easy life here.

She decided not to go home for Christmas but carefully sewed gifts for everyone from extra scraps—aprons for Lila and Iona, a neck scarf for Virgie Mae, and shirts for the men. She sent them to Atlantic Grove on the mailboat. She told herself that Aunt Velma needed her to help finish the extra holiday sewing, but the truth was that she would die if Papa ever treated her the cruel way he had treated Frank when he came back. Even Iona and Lila sometimes seemed standoffish in their letters. It seemed a person couldn't leave and go back and have it ever be the same.

In her letters to Lila and Papa, Eleanor took pains to write about how hard she was working to receive good marks. In her letters to Virgie Mae, she wrote about how her classmates dressed and what they talked about. It was only in her letters to Frank and Miss Rosalie that she wrote about her desire to be an independent woman.

One day in late spring Eleanor received a note from a boy named Ray Hamilton, a senior at the high school whom she had met with Aunt Velma at Centenary Methodist Church. It said:

Miss Eleanor Hill,

You are cordially invited to attend my graduation party at one-thirty in the afternoon at Dr. Hamilton's on June 5, 1915.

Yours truly,
Ray Hamilton

Ray's handwriting was flowing and bold, with three curlicues around the *R* in his name. When she had met him at Centenary, Ray wore his hair parted directly down the middle, with a rounded puff on each side above his ears, which stuck out. Ray's hand was damp and clammy when he shook hers, and Eleanor had quickly wiped her palm on her handkerchief as soon as he wasn't looking. He was dressed in very fine store-bought clothes, and as she and Aunt Velma left the church she had the feeling his eyes were following her.

As she studied the invitation, she reminded herself that she had not come to New Bern to court young men. "That is Dr. Hamilton's son!" Aunt Velma said, snatching the invitation. "They live in a magnificent home right on Front Street! I will write your papa and assure him there will be no dancing."

Naturally, Aunt Velma said that Eleanor would need a new dress for the party. She had several yards of blue-and-white dotted swiss left over from a dress order, and she and Eleanor sewed nonstop for two days. It was to be a sailor dress, with a broad detachable collar that tied in front, and a dropped waist. The sleeves came to Eleanor's elbows and had decorative ties.

"Turn around, now, Eleanor, let me pin this up." Eleanor, standing on a stool in the parlor, turned obediently as Aunt Velma, on her knees, pinned a hem in the new dress. Uncle Owen was in his easy chair, reading the *New Bern Tribune.*

"We'll put the hem just above your ankles," said Aunt Velma, her mouth full of pins. "That will be stylish but not vulgar."

"President Wilson has said that the sinking of the *Lusitania* will not force us into the war—he will pursue peace negotiations instead," said Uncle Owen from behind his paper to no one in particular.

Aunt Velma sat back on her heels. "All right, step back and let me see you."

The dress felt light and airy as a cloud as Eleanor twirled for Aunt Velma.

"Oh!" Aunt Velma breathed. "Ellie, you look like an angel. What do you think, Owen?"

"Me?" said Uncle Owen. "Well, I didn't vote for Wilson, but I admire his levelheadedness."

"No, Owen, I mean about Eleanor's dress."

He peeked from behind the *New Bern Tribune*. "Pretty is as pretty does," he said. Then he cleared his throat and added, "Beauty is only skin deep."

Eleanor smothered a smile. "Miss Rosalie likes Mr. Wilson, too, Uncle Owen," she said. "She likes his views on education."

"Miss Rosalie? Who's that?"

"A teacher of mine who lives in Wyoming now. Women in Wyoming are allowed to vote," Eleanor said. "She wrote that Wyoming even has had a woman governor."

"Imagine your aunt Velma going to cast a vote," said Uncle Owen. "Why, she'd vote for the one with the nicest smile or the best manners or the smartest-looking hat. Things that have nothing to do with what kind of president a man would be."

"I would not, Owen Winstead," Aunt Velma protested. "I married you, didn't I?" Eleanor bent her head to hide her smile.

"I rest my case," said Uncle Owen. "I had a very nice top hat while we were courting, and I know good and well that's the reason you married me."

"That is not the reason I married you," said Aunt Velma. "I married you because you had a horse and buggy. A girl's got to have a way to get around, doesn't she, Eleanor?" Aunt Velma winked at her.

"Yes, ma'am," Eleanor said, grinning.

"You may wear my gloves and take my parasol to the party," Aunt Velma said, changing the subject. "The cream of New Bern society will be there."

"I'm not going to be there," Uncle Owen pointed out dryly from behind his newspaper.

"It's a young people's social gathering, Owen, of course you won't be there. I meant the cream of New Bern youngsters."

"But my papa is only a fisherman," Eleanor pointed out.

"Never you mind," said Aunt Velma, putting the left-over pins back in her sewing box. "You're pretty enough and smart enough to hold your own with any eligible young man in this town." She stood up. "After all, Ray Hamilton has noticed you already. Now, go take that dress off. The hem is ready to be stitched."

Eleanor studied herself doubtfully in Aunt Velma's full-length mirror as she removed the dress. She was used to wearing a brassiere by now. She had gotten her "monthly visitor," as Lila called it, although she had heard other girls calling it "the curse." In the mirror, her body looked curvy, like a woman's. But her face still looked girlish and scared.

She liked the idea of dressing up and was curious to see

the inside of Dr. Hamilton's fine waterfront house. But she did not want to touch Ray's sweaty hand again or feel his eyes following her. Yet, how awful it would be if he did not notice her at all. She felt miserable and wonderful at the same time.

On the day of the party, Aunt Velma made Eleanor wash her hair. Then Eleanor set it in curling rags and sat on the back porch to let it dry in the sun. She was fit to be tied because Aunt Velma wouldn't let her do anything but sit and fan herself the entire morning for fear she'd break a sweat.

She read a chapter in a new book by Frances Hodgson Burnett called *The Secret Garden*. She wrote a letter to Virgie Mae describing all of the preparations for Ray Hamilton's party, which ended "To be continued . . ." She spent an hour working on a sweater she was knitting for little Caleb Junior. The morning seemed absolutely to drag by.

Finally Aunt Velma ironed the new dress. When Eleanor put it on, it was still warm and crisp. Her hair, released at last from the curling rags, fell in graceful waves across her cheeks, and Aunt Velma fussed with it until Eleanor was ready to scream.

"I can comb my own hair, Aunt Velma."

"A body can't see the back of her own head."

Then Aunt Velma disappeared for a short time and reappeared in a party dress herself. She was going as Eleanor's chaperone, and she said that all of the young people would have one.

Dr. Hamilton lived in a two-story, wood-shingled

Victorian house with two chimneys, which meant it might have as many as four fireplaces. Graceful steps led up to a porch that stretched across the entire front of the house and was held up by pairs of slim columns. A room in the shape of a half-moon jutted out from one side on the first floor. Above the porch on the second floor Eleanor noticed a small eight-sided room with windows on every side. She was captivated by that room and thought to herself that if she didn't like the party she would escape there and watch the river.

When they rang the bell, the door was opened by a silent, smiling Negro woman.

"Harriet, send the guests to the parlor!" sang a female voice from upstairs.

"Oh my, are we the first to arrive?" asked Aunt Velma.

"Yes'm," said Harriet as she showed them into the front hall.

"Lord, one should never be early to a party," said Aunt Velma.

Eleanor stood rooted to the floor, staring at the plush rug with beautiful intricate patterns at her feet. She wanted to kneel and examine it more closely but felt sure that wouldn't be polite. To the right of the entrance hall was a dining room with a round table and sideboard, both laden with food, crystal, and silver. To the left was a large parlor with an enormous multicolored rug, scattered arrangements of brocade chairs, and a grand piano whose black-lacquered wood shone.

In front of them was the most magnificent staircase Eleanor had ever seen. Several wide burnished stairs led up to a landing, where a vase of cascading pink and purple flowers stood on a smooth, dark table with dainty legs. Perched next to the flower vase in a position of honor was something Eleanor had never seen in a private home—a slim, black telephone with its bell-shaped earpiece hanging on a hook.

"This way please, ma'am."

"Law, I could die. I just can't believe we're the first ones," Aunt Velma repeated as they followed Harriet into the front parlor. Just then, Dr. Hamilton and his wife, stylishly dressed, swept down the staircase with their children following, including Ray Junior, who wore sky-blue seersucker slacks, suspenders, and a starched white shirt with full sleeves.

Ray's ears turned red the moment he saw Eleanor, and his eyes darted quickly away. Eleanor looked away, too, but sneaked another peek at him a moment later and caught him watching her again. A crowd of people had arrived and stood in the front hall, and Aunt Velma grabbed Eleanor's arm and marched her forward.

". . . and I'd like you to meet my niece, Miss Eleanor Hill. She made the acquaintance of your son Ray at Centenary."

"How do you do?" Eleanor murmured as she curtseyed to Ray's parents the way Aunt Velma had taught her. She remembered pretending to curtsey on the beach in Atlantic Grove, and here she was, only this time it was real. "You have a beautiful home. Thank you for inviting me."

Ray's parents were gracious, but Eleanor suddenly felt miserable in her homemade dress and wished she hadn't come. She didn't belong here. The other young people wore fine clothes and came from beautiful houses like this one. They went sailing just for fun, not to fish, and had more than one pair of shoes. Worst of all, Aunt Velma acted as if Eleanor were something for sale, a bolt of cloth or a stylish hat.

But just as she was ready to give in to the impulse to run home, Ray Junior approached her, took her hand, and shook it formally. His hand was just as clammy as she remembered, but it didn't bother her as much as she thought it would.

"You came! I was afraid you wouldn't," he said in a rush. "I thought because you didn't know many people..." He looked at his feet.

"It was so kind of you to invite me."

"I remembered you from Centenary. Do you enjoy the young people's group there?"

"Yes, very much," she said. She glimpsed Aunt Velma in the dining room telling a white-aproned servant to add another slice of pound cake to her already laden plate. She gave Eleanor a sneaky-looking smile and winked at her.

"How about a glass of punch?" Ray asked.

"That would be nice." She followed him into the dining room, where bubbly red punch filled an enormous crystal bowl. Floating in the punch were strawberries and chunks of ice. Ray said something to one of the servants and then took Eleanor's arm.

"Would you like to sit on the porch?" he asked.

"I thought we were getting punch," said Eleanor.

"The servant will bring it to us."

"Well, there's no need. I can get my own." Eleanor felt embarrassed at the idea of someone serving her when she could perfectly well do it herself.

"Nonsense, that's what they're here for." As Ray steered Eleanor through the crowded parlor, they nearly bumped into Gertrude, Uncle Owen's niece, who had been so taken with Frank at Lila's wedding. Gertrude's spit curls were gone now, Eleanor noticed, and her hair was fashionably bobbed.

"Well, hello," said Gertrude. "I remember you from that charming country wedding. Lenore, is it?"

"Eleanor."

"Eleanor, you must tell me about your darling brother Frank. Where is he these days?"

"He's in San Francisco. He owns a motor company now."

"How exciting! He had the markings of success, in my mind. Is he married?"

Eleanor suppressed a smile. "No, he's not."

"Maybe you could catch the next train to San Francisco," suggested Ray with what Eleanor thought was a wicked smile.

"I couldn't do that, Ray, that would be chasing a man, and I'm not the type of girl to do such a thing."

Ray laughed out loud. "Well, then, what type of girl are you?"

"Well, if you don't know, I won't tell you," said Gertrude, making a face.

Ray quickly guided Eleanor to a pair of French doors that opened onto a side porch. Aunt Velma, talking with another chaperone, waved daintily as Eleanor passed.

She and Ray sat in two wicker rocking chairs on the side porch. "It's a fine view, isn't it?" Ray said. Eleanor looked out. The Hamiltons' large, manicured lawn sloped down to a stone wall enclosing their property. Beyond the wall was Front Street and the Neuse River, sparkling in the sunlight. Ray pointed to a massive live oak down near the stone wall. "I always loved to sit in that tree and watch the boats."

A moment later Harriet brought a tray with their punch. A strawberry floated in each cup. Eleanor murmured a "thank-you."

"Harriet," said Ray, "why is there no ice in our punch?"

"We run out, sir," said Harriet.

Ray stood up. "Please excuse me, Miss Hill."

Before Eleanor could protest that having ice wasn't important, Ray was gone. The wicker chair creaked softly as she rocked. She could hear the low rumble of voices inside the house but felt removed and peaceful and surrounded by beauty.

It seemed she had been there only a moment when Ray returned. "I telephoned the ice company," he said, settling himself in the rocker. "The wagon should be here directly."

He began to tell Eleanor about himself. His graduating class consisted of fifteen young men and seven young ladies. Next year he planned to attend college at the University of North Carolina. His parents then wanted him to go on to medical school and become a doctor, like his father.

"My, you certainly have plans," said Eleanor. She sipped her cup of punch in what she hoped was a ladylike manner. The floating strawberry kept bumping her lip. It would be useful right now to know the proper way to eat a strawberry floating in a cup of punch. She was trying to memorize every minute of what was happening, every word of the conversation, to describe to Virgie Mae.

"Perhaps you'd like to go for a ride in our automobile some fine day," Ray was saying.

"Oh, you have an automobile?"

"Yes, do you like riding in them?"

"Oh yes, and driving, too," Eleanor said.

"You drive?"

"Just a little," she said quickly, hoping she hadn't shocked him. She glanced at him through her eyelashes. His ears were still scarlet, and there were tiny beads of sweat on his upper lip.

"Well, then, I would like to see a demonstration of your driving ability," he said. "I don't meet many girls who know how to drive. In fact, I believe you're the first."

"I would love that," Eleanor said, hoping her voice didn't squeak. She'd always wondered what Lila saw in skinny old Caleb, but now the attentions of this young man made her feel so special it hardly mattered what she saw in him.

They both looked up quickly at the sound of a wagon approaching. Eleanor took advantage of the moment to plunge her fingers into the punch, grab the floating strawberry, and pop it in her mouth.

The wagon driver pulled back on the reins. "Whoa, Jeremy. Did you order another block of ice, Mr. Hamilton?"

The young man spoke formally, and his voice had a slightly foreign lilt to it.

Ray stood and gestured up the alley beside the house. "Yes, take it on around back, please."

"Yes, sir." The young man snapped the mule's reins. Watching him, Eleanor had an eerie sense of familiarity. She stood up and found herself walking to the porch railing to get a better look at him.

The young man nodded at her and lifted his cap. As he did so, Eleanor recognized the mischievous face, the dark, curly eyelashes, and the fearless smile of the boy who dove from the crow's-nest the day she arrived in New Bern. And she could tell when his eyes met hers, and by the way he pulled on the reins to slow the mule, that he recognized her, too.

"Miss Hill," Ray was saying, "is there something wrong?"

"Oh no," Eleanor replied. "I believe I feel a little faint because of the heat."

"Here, we'll have this young man stop and give you a piece of ice for your forehead."

"Oh no, I'll be fine, really."

"I insist. Young man! Stop, please, we need some ice for the young lady. She's feeling faint."

The young man pulled on the reins and jumped down from the wagon, then ran around back. Using a pickax, he chopped off a chunk of ice, gallantly wrapped it in his handkerchief, and handed the bundle up over the porch railing to Eleanor.

"Allow me," he said, his hand brushing Eleanor's.

"Oh, I can't take your handkerchief," Eleanor protested.

"Please think nothing of it," the young man said.

He looked as if he might say more, but Ray stepped closer. "Thank you, she'll be fine now."

The young man nodded and swung back up onto the wagon, which lumbered behind the house and out of Eleanor's sight. She sat down in the wicker rocker and held the ice to her forehead.

"Are you feeling any better?" Ray asked solicitously.

"A little," Eleanor said.

"Ellie!" Aunt Velma came out on the porch with a plateful of food. "You haven't come in to eat a thing. Ray Hamilton, fine young gentleman that he is, must stay here with you until you eat every bite."

"Oh please, Aunt Velma, I'm fine," Eleanor said. This was so embarrassing.

"Mrs. Winstead," Ray was saying politely, "Eleanor has agreed to go for a ride in our family automobile one Sunday afternoon, and I would be honored if you would act as our chaperone."

"I would be delighted!" Aunt Velma was so enthusiastic that Eleanor blushed.

As Eleanor listened to their conversation, she lowered the damp handkerchief from her forehead and spread out a corner so she could see the monogram. "NVG." She wondered what it stood for.

⇒ *Two Suitors* ⇐

Eleanor did not show "NVG's" handkerchief to Aunt Velma or Uncle Owen. Should she try to return it or wait for the young man to seek her out? He might not know her name or how to find her. If she tried to find him and give it back, she might see him again. But returning it might imply that she was *not* interested in him. This was all very confusing. Since she could not decide what to do, she put the handkerchief in her tea tin, tucked between letters from Lila and Frank, and wrote Miss Rosalie for advice.

July 2, 1915

Dear Miss Rosalie,

The last month of high school went very well. You will be so proud of me—I won the award for the most outstanding student in Bookkeeping. In English I memorized a number of poems by Emily Dickinson. The senior class put on an end-of-the-year production of A Midsummer Night's Dream *by William Shakespeare, and I helped with the costumes. Next year I will be a junior—can you believe it?*

I recently attended a graduation party at one of the loveliest homes in New Bern. There was an abundance of food, punch, beautiful flowers, lovely crystal and china, and white linen tablecloths. When you were my teacher I used to daydream about going to elegant teas in New Bern, never thinking it would someday come true.

In the evenings I listen to musical programs and news about the war on the crystal set with Uncle Owen and Aunt Velma. Do you remember Nat Taylor, the boy who put the sand crab in my desk? Lila writes me that he lied about his age and has joined the French Army and gone to Paris! Lila says that Nat is too lazy to be much of a student or a waterman and she reckons he won't be much of a soldier, either.

I have a question about etiquette that I hope you will be able to answer. When a young man very gallantly offers his handkerchief to a young lady in distress, what is the proper course of action? Should the young lady endeavor to return the handkerchief? Or should she wait for the young man to reclaim it? If the young lady keeps such an item, am I guessing correctly that it means she would be receptive to attentions from that young man?

> *Your faithful student,*
> *Eleanor Hill*

While Eleanor waited for Miss Rosalie's reply, Ray Hamilton invited her for the promised ride in his family's automobile on a Sunday afternoon in July, right after church. It was a sunny, bright day, and the air was filled with the scent of Aunt Velma's roses and camellias. Aunt Velma tried four outfits before she settled on her green gabardine suit and cape as the perfect attire for chaperoning a drive. Eleanor wore a plain navy school skirt and white blouse and refused the broad straw hat Aunt Velma wanted her to wear.

Eleanor and Aunt Velma sat on the porch swing to wait for Ray. Uncle Owen, in the porch rocker, offered Aunt Velma advice about the upcoming ride. "I recommend keeping your arms inside the automobile."

"If I see someone I know, Owen, I will at least wave."

"And do not attempt to stand up while the vehicle is moving."

"Why on earth would I want to do that?"

Eleanor thought Aunt Velma would faint with excitement when Ray arrived in his yellow Packard. There were broad white stripes on the tires, and the green leather seats were so shiny that Eleanor was afraid when she sat down she might slide right onto the floorboards. The car looked like a tropical bird compared to Frank's sensible Model T, although she knew her brother would drive a Packard if he could.

Ray wore a driving helmet with goggles that emphasized his protruding ears and clumps of hair. Eleanor was sure every person on Johnson Street was peeking at him and the Packard between their parlor drapes.

"Well, hello!" she said. "Do you have helmets and goggles for Aunt Velma and me, too?"

"I'm sorry to say I have only one extra pair," said Ray.

"Aunt Velma, you should wear them."

"Oh no, I wouldn't hear of it," said Aunt Velma, as they descended the porch steps. "I have my hat."

So Eleanor took the helmet and snapped it snugly under her chin. She placed a picnic basket with egg-salad sandwiches and several Mason jars filled with lemonade in the backseat and climbed up front.

"We can ride down to the Glenburnie Park Pavilion and have lunch by the river," said Ray. "They're launching a hot-air balloon today."

Uncle Owen circled the Packard twice, examining all the details, before opening a back door and helping Aunt Velma climb in. "Under no circumstances are you to let my wife drive this car, Ray. Velma, I don't see much sense in wearing that little hat since it is likely to blow off."

Aunt Velma clamped her hand on the hat. "I'll just keep hold of it as we go."

"I've been thinking of buying a car," Uncle Owen told Ray. "But I want to see if the price comes down any more."

"Mr. Winstead," said Ray, "would you care to accompany us?"

"Certainly not," said Aunt Velma. "If he came, we'd have nowhere to put the picnic basket."

"Why, thank you kindly, Ray, I would be pleased as punch," said Uncle Owen, climbing in back beside Aunt Velma. "Set that picnic basket on your lap, Velma."

Eleanor smiled at Ray apologetically, but he made a grand gesture with his arms that seemed to say "The more the merrier!" and climbed in the car beside her. Eleanor had decided she would only drive the elegant Packard if Ray offered. She watched carefully as he cranked the engine, following steps similar to the ones Frank had taught her. The engine caught, and the car started to vibrate.

"Ready?" Ray, in his helmet, turned to look at her.

"Ready!" they all replied, and he released the hand brake, pressed on the accelerator pedal, and released the clutch. The car leaped forward. Aunt Velma grabbed her hat.

Ray was not as good a driver as Frank. He was hesitant about taking turns, and a few times when they stopped at intersections the car died altogether. But it was a lovely day, with such a nice breeze down by the water that Eleanor took off the goggles and helmet and let her hair blow free. First they drove down Front Street and past the docks, then headed out to Glenburnie, where there was a fairgrounds and a pavilion. Aunt Velma waved eagerly at every soul she saw, whether she knew that person or not. They watched as a famous balloonist ascended in what was supposedly the world's largest hot-air balloon. The ascension took place with great fanfare, and then he made a daring parachute jump from five thousand feet.

Afterward Eleanor spread a blanket on the grass by the river under the shade of a willow tree, and they ate the sandwiches and drank the lemonade as they watched people in their church finery walk by on their Sunday afternoon strolls. Many people stopped to admire the Packard, which pleased Ray. He complimented Eleanor several times on her egg salad. Then Uncle Owen expressed his opinions about the United States entering the war and asked Ray for his thoughts on the subject.

"Owen, it's not polite to ask the young man political questions," Aunt Velma protested.

"Why not? I just want to know what he thinks."

"My mother says I have a surgeon's hands and I should not go to war, but my father says if the United States joins the war the Hamiltons will participate," said Ray. "I have plans to go to college at the University of North Carolina next fall."

"I see," said Uncle Owen.

"Owen," said Aunt Velma, with a wink at Eleanor, "please help me get up. I would like to take a stroll."

"Now?" said Uncle Owen. "We just ate. I would like to let my lunch digest."

"Come on, Owen, I feel like taking a walk."

Uncle Owen sighed heavily and got to his feet, then pulled Aunt Velma up. "You never walk at home, Velma, why would you want to walk now?"

"Enjoy yourselves," she called to Eleanor and Ray as she firmly hooked her arm through Uncle Owen's and started across the grass. Uncle Owen's complaining voice became fainter as she dragged him farther away.

"Well," said Ray, smiling at Eleanor.

"That's a deep subject." Eleanor met Ray's eyes, laughed nervously, and then looked down, smoothing her skirt over her ankles. She looked back up again.

"Your aunt and uncle are very pleasant people," Ray offered.

"They've been very kind to me."

"Well, a girl like you deserves to be treated kindly." Eleanor noticed there was sweat on his upper lip, just like at the party.

"This lemonade is extremely delicious," said Ray. As

he upturned the tin cup, there was an angry buzzing sound, and two bees came soaring out of it.

"Whoa!" Ray leaped to his feet, dropped the cup on the grass, and flailed his arms, trying to knock them away. The bees flew away at last, but not before stinging him on his cheek and his finger.

"Ray, are you all right?"

"I'm allergic to bee stings!"

"You don't mean to say you swell up like a blowfish?"

"I do," he said in a shaky voice. "We'd best head home."

"Let me fetch Aunt Velma and Uncle Owen," Eleanor said. "Why don't you just rest until we get back?"

"All right," he said faintly. He lay on his back on the blanket and closed his eyes.

By the time Eleanor returned with her aunt and uncle, one of Ray's eyes had swollen shut, and his hand looked like a boxing glove. While Aunt Velma made a terrible fuss, Uncle Owen pulled the tobacco from one of his cigars and caked it over the bites to draw out the poison. Ray was close to fainting from fear of his imminent death. Eleanor quickly packed up the lunch and herded the three of them into the Packard. Without even thinking, she put Aunt Velma and Uncle Owen in back, Ray in the passenger seat, and climbed behind the steering wheel.

"Mercy, Eleanor, what are you doing?" exclaimed Aunt Velma. She was leaning over the front seat, fanning Ray with her hat.

"Look at his eye, Aunt Velma, he can't see to drive," said Eleanor. "So I'm going to." She set the spark lever, opened the throttle, and ran to the front to crank the engine.

"You can't drive!" said Aunt Velma. "Can you?"

"I hope I can remember how." Eleanor opened the throttle further while holding down the clutch with her right foot, and the Packard started to grind.

"I ought to drive," said Uncle Owen loudly.

"You've never driven a car in your life," Aunt Velma replied.

"Driving is a mechanical talent that comes naturally to men," said Uncle Owen. "Besides, what will people think, with a slip of a girl behind the wheel and me in the backseat?"

Eleanor ignored him. She drove as fast as she dared back into New Bern. When she took turns the tires squealed, and so did Aunt Velma. The Packard had three speeds, so she moved the change-speed lever to the highest one and left it there as they chugged down Middle Street.

"Watch out for that carriage!" Uncle Owen called. Eleanor veered around a horse and carriage starting out of a side street. The horse reared with a neigh of alarm, and the carriage stopped so quickly that two of the riders in the back were thrown halfway into the front seat.

"Bee sting!" Aunt Velma called to onlookers as they charged by.

At last Eleanor screeched to a halt in front of Ray's house. She had the car door open before the engine died, and she grabbed her skirt and ran up the steps to his front door. Harriet, whom she remembered from the party, answered the door.

"We need Dr. Hamilton!" Eleanor said. "Ray has been stung by bees and is all swollen up."

"Lord have mercy!" Harriet ran down the hall calling Dr. Hamilton. A moment later, Ray's father rushed out to the car with his dinner napkin still in his hand. He quickly examined the swelling, thanked Eleanor, and took his son next-door to his office.

"I hope everything is all right," Eleanor called to Ray, who waved with his swollen hand while holding the other over his eye. She stood uncertainly with her aunt and uncle on the sidewalk until Dr. Hamilton came back out of his office, the sleeves of his white shirt rolled to his elbows.

"The tobacco was a good thing," he said. "I think he'll be fine in a few hours. He says he will send you a note soon."

Eleanor nodded with relief, and then she and Aunt Velma and Uncle Owen started walking home.

"I certainly hope the driving doesn't have a negative effect on his interest in you," Aunt Velma said after a block or so.

"Indeed," said Uncle Owen when Eleanor did not reply.

As they turned onto Johnson Street, she added, "He is a very good catch, Eleanor. Why, if you married him, you would most likely end up living in that beautiful house on Front Street. That's nothing to sneeze at."

They climbed the front porch steps, and Aunt Velma and Uncle Owen, neither of whom were used to quite so much strolling or excitement, went upstairs to take a nap. Eleanor was feeling restless and sat outside in the porch swing. With the balls of her feet just touching the porch floor, she pushed herself gently back and forth.

She'd been so worried about Ray's bee stings that she hadn't thought about the sheer joy of driving the Packard at top speed until now. She brushed off Aunt Velma's concern about Ray calling on her again. If he gave up on her that easily, so be it. *I am not here in New Bern to find a husband*, she reminded herself. *I am here to get an education and become an independent woman.*

She had just reached up to comb her tangled hair with her fingers when she saw a young man round the corner onto Johnson Street. He walked slowly, as if unfamiliar with the neighborhood. His cap was at an angle, and he was dressed so stylishly that Eleanor almost didn't recognize him. He carried a bouquet of wildflowers.

Eleanor remained rocking in the swing, but held her breath as her heart began to thud against her rib cage. As he drew nearer, and she became surer of who he was, and whom he planned to visit, her heart skipped several beats. She feared it might leap right out of her chest and lie there flopping like a fish on the porch floorboards. She lay both hands firmly at the base of her throat just in case. Her skin felt hot against her fingers.

He reached the steps. His curly black eyelashes framed his liquid brown eyes. His nose was straight and sharp, his lips full and smooth, his skin darker than Eleanor's. When he removed his cap and bowed slightly she saw his dark hair was wavy and shiny. "I believe you are in possession of one of my handkerchiefs." His voice had a lilt, and there was a smile in his eyes.

"Yes," she managed to say.

"I hope you will do me the honor of keeping it as a token of my esteem," he said. "My name is Niccolo Vespucci Garibaldi. 'Vespucci' is for the famous Italian adventurer who discovered South America." Then he added, "My friends call me Nick."

Niccolo Vespucci Garibaldi. "NVG." At last she had a name to attach to the face that had been in her memory since her first day in New Bern.

He held out the bouquet for her to take. She wondered if he had picked the flowers from the side of the road— there were daisies, Queen Anne's lace, goldenrod, and bluets. She took the bouquet and smiled. "I'm pleased to meet you. My name is Eleanor Hill."

"I know." When he smiled his teeth were remarkably white next to his olive skin. "And you come from Atlantic Grove, and you are living with your aunt Velma and uncle Owen Winstead while you attend New Bern Graded School."

"My, you're the detective."

"Yes, I am. I would be honored if you would accompany me to the picture show at the Masonic Theater next Saturday afternoon," he continued. "*Birth of a Nation* will be showing. Since my family is relatively new to this country, I am especially interested in seeing this film showing the history of America. I hear it is three hours long!"

Eleanor was aware that talking with him was wrong. She did not know his family or any mutual friends. She knew vaguely that Aunt Velma and Uncle Owen did not socialize with people from other countries. She should not have accepted the flowers. She should go inside at once and get the handkerchief from her tea tin and return it to him.

"I would love to," she heard herself say. "Of course, my aunt Velma must accompany us as a chaperone."

"Of course," he said, carefully pronouncing the sound of the *o* in "course."

Eleanor imagined herself sitting with Nick in the Masonic Theater in the dark, and Aunt Velma seated discreetly a few rows behind them, beaming with her matronly approval. But at that point the daydream stopped because Eleanor knew Aunt Velma would never approve.

"I have been thinking of you ever since the day I saw you on the mailboat," Nick was saying.

"Are you still driving the ice wagon?"

"Yes. My uncle owns the ice plant, and I have moved here to help him out and learn about running a business. My parents live in Richmond, Virginia, where they own a dry-goods establishment. What I really want to have is a business of my own. I am saving my money to open a haberdashery shop."

"That's very enterprising."

"That's the wonderful thing about America. Everyone's dreams can come true." He smiled again. Eleanor lay her cool fingers on her hot cheeks and looked away.

"So. You will keep my handkerchief?" Keeping his handkerchief would send him a message that she was interested in a courtship. She should say no and return it.

"Yes, I will," she said.

Nothing but a Good Name

"The Masonic Theater! And you kept his handkerchief!" Uncle Owen snapped the newspaper shut. "A poor girl has nothing if she has lost her good name."

Aunt Velma, on the parlor couch, employed her black lace fan so vigorously that the gray hair framing her face puffed out in one-two rhythm. "Dr. Hamilton's son is interested in you and you kept the handkerchief of a perfect stranger?"

"But, Aunt Velma—" Eleanor sighed. She'd waited three days to broach the subject, knowing they would object, but this was worse than she had expected.

"And an immigrant at that!" Uncle Owen exploded. "He probably doesn't even speak good English. And Lord knows, he's probably a Catholic! I forbid it." Uncle Owen sounded to Eleanor like Papa when she drove Frank's car. "Now, you march upstairs and write that scallywag and return his handkerchief."

To keep herself from saying or doing anything that she might regret, Eleanor mumbled, "Yessir," and left the room. She clomped loudly up the stairs so they would know how she felt. Why had she told them anything?

Aunt Velma and Uncle Owen were rejecting Nick for all the wrong reasons. To tell the truth, Eleanor wasn't exactly sure why she herself had such innate trust in Nick or why she was so drawn to him. After all, she'd only seen him three times in her life. But she did and she was.

What did she care if his family came from Italy? Her family came from Atlantic Grove. Sometimes it seemed just as far away. Besides, she wasn't thinking of *marrying* him. She wasn't thinking of marrying anyone. She just wanted to go to the picture show.

Upstairs in her room, she got out a sheet of writing paper. Frank was the only person who would understand. "Dear Frank," she wrote,

> *I have been invited to view* Birth of a Nation, *but Aunt Velma and Uncle Owen do not want me to go with the young man who has asked me. Uncle Owen says he's an immigrant and maybe even a Catholic.*
>
> *But he brought me flowers and he dresses very stylishly and is a perfect gentleman. He is very enterprising—he wants to have his own business. And he has the loveliest brown eyes, although I know a girl should not attach importance to such things. What do you think of this? What harm is there in going to the picture show?*

She finished the letter and sealed it quickly so no one else would read it. Then she got out a second sheet of paper. She dipped her pen in the inkwell and blotted it carefully. She wrote "Dear Mr. Garibaldi" and stopped, her pen poised above the paper.

She remembered how he had bowed when he saw her on the porch. She wanted to feel his feathery eyelashes under her fingertip and run the backs of her fingers over his smooth olive cheeks.

"Have you finished the letter?" Aunt Velma's voice from the doorway startled her, and a drop of ink plopped onto the page. She could feel heat rising up her neck.

"No, I have to start over—there's an inkblot."

Aunt Velma sat on the bed and folded her arms across her stomach. "I'll wait while you write it and mail it myself."

Eleanor wadded the paper into a ball and dropped it into the wastebasket. Slowly she took out another sheet. She could feel Aunt Velma's eyes on her back. Was this the same Aunt Velma who had hugged her the first day of school, listened to her recite *Thanatopsis,* and cut her hair in a stylish bob? Who had spent hours on her dress for Ray's graduation party? The silence behind her was heavy. Slowly she wrote "Dear Mr. Garibaldi" again.

"Eleanor, did anyone ever tell you that your mama and papa eloped?" When Eleanor turned in her chair she saw that Aunt Velma was staring at her with trembling cheeks.

"No, ma'am." Eleanor put down her pen.

"Your mama—my little sister—was such a beauty, so refined and charming, she could have had herself any man she wanted. But she fell in love with a fisherman. When she told me she planned to run off with your papa I tried to stop her. She wanted me to help her pack, and instead I locked her in a closet for the whole afternoon. But she was so crazy about John Hill that three weeks later they tried again, and that time she didn't tell me. They jumped on the mailboat, and by the time it docked in Atlantic Grove they were married. Your mother was fourteen."

As Aunt Velma told the story, Eleanor imagined her mother in the dark closet, banging on the door, while Papa stood at the dock waiting for her, watching the sun drop behind the trees. She imagined a young Aunt Velma in the kitchen, with the closet key safe in her skirt pocket, helping their mother make supper as the sky outside grew red.

"Uncle Owen had a horse and carriage and a good job with the railroad. When I married him I moved up in the world. When your mama married your papa she moved down."

"She did not! How can you say that about Papa!"

"And believe you me, I'd lock *you* in a closet, too, if I thought you were planning to marry down. Your mama was too fine a girl to waste herself on the wrong man, and so are you." Aunt Velma's chin shook, and Eleanor saw that she was about to cry. Angry at first, Eleanor suddenly realized that Aunt Velma had loved Mama just as Eleanor loved Lila, and that she had missed her terribly when she went away and married. Eleanor hadn't thought Caleb was good enough for Lila, just as Aunt Velma thought Papa wasn't good enough for Mama. Then it occurred to her that Aunt Velma might be the one person able to tell her what her mama was really like.

"Tell me about Mama," Eleanor said, folding her arms over the back of her desk chair.

Aunt Velma crossed her legs and leaned on her elbow

on the bed. "Well, Annis was the baby, a little bit spoiled, and very pretty, prettier than me. I was the practical one, always ready for school with my homework done. Annis could never find her shoes or her hair bow, and she would often run out the door and leave her schoolbooks on the kitchen table. Once she learned to read, Mama said she left this world. The house could have burned down, and she wouldn't have noticed."

"She was smart in school?" Eleanor got up from the desk and lay on her stomach across the bed, facing Aunt Velma, her chin in her hands.

"Oh yes, her marks were better than mine, especially in Composition. She was good at drawing a likeness of things, too. Annis had such a way of looking at the world that when she and I talked things over at the end of the day, that day always seemed to have been better. But in my opinion she should not have read all those books. They put highfalutin ideas in her head. She was full of passion and romance, and the truth is, life is a hard row to hoe."

"I wish I had known her," said Eleanor.

"I always felt I had to take care of her." Aunt Velma's chin was shaking again. "Mama had all the boys to worry about, so I worried about Annis. And then she went off, and John Hill was supposed to take care of her, but he didn't."

"But Mama and Papa loved each other!"

Aunt Velma sat up sharply. "Sometimes love just isn't enough." She pulled a lace handkerchief from her bosom and blew her nose. "Now, let's get that letter written."

Eleanor remembered Iona, so sad and severe, standing in the cemetery after Lila's wedding and saying that

Mama was not meant to be a fisherman's wife. It made her heart ache to think about her mama's short, sad life.

Feeling as if she was betraying Papa, she dipped her pen in the inkwell and wiped the nib carefully. She wrote the letter to Nick, saying it was with great regret that she must return his handkerchief and refuse his kind invitation to the Masonic Theater. When she was finished, and the ink was dry, she gave the letter and the handkerchief to Aunt Velma, who read the letter line by line and pronounced it "satisfactory."

Now she would never see him again.

A week crept by, hot and sultry, and Eleanor kept a towel in the sewing room to prevent dampening the articles of clothing she worked on. Aunt Velma complained about her eyes and was doing less and less of the work, leaving more for Eleanor.

To her surprise, Eleanor received a note from Ray Hamilton.

Miss Eleanor Hill,

Please do me the honor of accompanying me to view Birth of a Nation *on Saturday, August 28, at the Masonic Theater at 2:15 p.m.*

Sincerely,
Ray Hamilton

Aunt Velma and Uncle Owen seemed pleased as punch for her to go. "So it's not acceptable for me to go to the Masonic Theater with Niccolo Garibaldi, but it's perfectly fine for me to go with Ray Hamilton, is that it?" Eleanor confronted them both at the dinner table.

"You explain it, Owen," said Aunt Velma, patting her lips with her napkin.

"A good name is more to be valued than silver or gold," intoned Uncle Owen. "Let us bow our heads and ask the Lord's blessing."

Eleanor was silent the rest of the meal.

"I'm tickled pink that driving his car hasn't cooled Ray's feelings for you." Aunt Velma stirred sugar into her coffee and beamed at Eleanor.

"You're lucky we stopped any dalliance you might have had with that Italian scallywag." Uncle Owen pushed back from the table, took his napkin from his belt, and tossed it beside his plate. He went into the parlor and opened the newspaper.

Eleanor stood and began to stack the dishes without speaking. She had to admit that all the crowd at the New Bern Fourth of July celebration had been anticipating the arrival of *Birth of a Nation,* and she very much wanted to go. She had also thought a great deal about Aunt Velma's story of her mother's elopement. Perhaps her mother *had* been unhappy. Perhaps she *could* have had a better life. Eleanor was determined that she would try once more to see Ray Hamilton's good points.

Saturday dawned clear but windy. Ray Hamilton was dressed stylishly in gray flannel slacks when he rang the bell after lunch. The theater was only a few blocks away, and they easily could walk. Ray told Eleanor that his elderly neighbor Mrs. Maple would be attending the film and would be pleased to act as their chaperone. Aunt Velma and Uncle Owen agreed that this would be fine.

"Eleanor, be sure and take your umbrella," said Aunt Velma. "Fannie Lupton down the street has a telephone, you know, and her cousin Livy called from Morehead City this morning saying the winds are blowing a gale and the water is high."

"Nonsense," said Uncle Owen from behind the newspaper. "It says right here the Weather Bureau has no indication of any disturbances, and the rest of the week will be calm and balmy."

"I don't put much stock in that Weather Bureau," said Aunt Velma. "They completely missed that big hurricane that tore through from Galveston in 1902."

"That was more than a dozen years ago, Velma, and I reckon I put more stock in the Weather Bureau than in Fannie Lupton's cousin Livy," said Uncle Owen.

"What have you got against Livy, I'd like to know? Why don't we tie up the porch swing just in case?"

"Because the Weather Bureau says there isn't going to be a storm."

Eleanor took the umbrella, and she and Ray went out into the wind, leaving Aunt Velma and Uncle Owen arguing in the parlor. "Well, if it rains, the picture show is a good place to be," Ray said with a smile as they headed down the block.

"I'm sure there are no bees inside the Masonic Theater," she said with a wink.

"Very funny, Miss Hill. Mrs. Maple said she would

meet us at the theater. How about a Pepsi-Cola before-hand?"

"All right."

Ray showed her to a table next to the window at Bradham's Drugstore, and they watched the wind tear hats from people's heads and billow women's skirts like sails. They laughed at a man chasing his bowler as it rolled down the road.

This is just what Lila and Caleb did when they became engaged, Eleanor thought. How grand Lila's date had sounded to her back then. Yet here she was, sitting in Bradham's Drugstore with an eligible young man, sipping her very own Pepsi-Cola, but she didn't feel the way she'd expected to.

By the time they arrived at the theater, clouds had rolled in, and the wind had increased. "Looks like cousin Livy has won out over the Weather Bureau," Ray commented as he paid five cents for their tickets. "I do believe it's going to storm."

"Well, it can storm away for the next three hours. We'll be having a lovely time."

The exterior of the theater was built to look Arabian or Spanish, with mock minarets and adobe walls. The lobby had an ornate chandelier and red carpet, and in the theater itself there was an orchestra pit up front and gilded opera boxes on either side of the stage. The curtain was painted with a chariot-race scene from the story of Ben Hur.

Ray ushered Eleanor down a row of richly upholstered, comfortable seats, and she let her fingertips graze the fine fabric before sitting down. Mrs. Maple waved discreetly from the row right behind them, smiling. Eleanor had a feeling she had promised Ray she would chaperone as little as possible.

The curtain rose, the lights dimmed, and then, instead of music from the usual lone piano player, the theater was completely filled with a recording of a full orchestra! Eleanor was transfixed by the film—why, sometimes hundreds of people were on the screen at once. Ray whispered that this was the first film ever made in which the mood of the music had been specially recorded to reflect the action on the screen. Eleanor was so overwhelmed that she barely noticed when he took her hand in his.

"In a few weeks I will leave New Bern," he said when the film ended, "to attend the University of North Carolina."

"My, it's warm," she said. Ray's hand was clammy, and she disengaged her hand from his and fanned herself with her program. "Wasn't that just a spectacular film?" The theater lights came up. Now that the music had stopped, she could hear the wind howling outside.

"May I hope to correspond with you once I am in Chapel Hill?"

"Oh, certainly." Eleanor was flustered and glanced across the theater, only to find herself looking directly into a pair of bold brown eyes with dark, curly eyelashes. She gasped out loud and ducked down.

"Eleanor, are you all right?"

"Yes, just getting my umbrella."

She sat up slowly, hardly daring to look back in Nick's direction, but it was too late. He had seen her and was holding his cap in front of his heart with a look of despair and betrayal.

"Good, we'll correspond."

"What?" Eleanor tore her gaze away from Nick and tried to focus on what Ray was saying.

"We'll write each other," he repeated.

"Of course." She looked back in Nick's direction, but he had melted into the crowd.

Suddenly one of New Bern's volunteer firemen shoved the heavy stage curtain aside and ran onstage. "Folks, it looks like we got a hurricane coming our way. Please leave the theater in an orderly fashion and take cover as soon as you can."

With a buzz of anxious conversation, the crowd streamed toward the aisles and exits. As Ray and Eleanor stood and turned toward the lobby, Mrs. Maple rose to her feet, her face tight and scared.

"Let me help you, Mrs. Maple." Ray took her hand and led her into the aisle.

"Thank you, Ray," she said. "I'm not too steady on my feet these days, and it sounds awfully bad out there."

Ray looked through the lobby doors at the driving rain and turned to Eleanor. "Miss Hill, why don't you wait here where it's dry, and I'll come back and get you after I walk Mrs. Maple home?"

"That's silly, Ray. Mrs. Maple lives two doors down from you, and I live in the other direction. You take her and get inside. I'll get home all right."

"I can't bear to think of you walking home by yourself."

"I'll be fine. I've lived through many a hurricane in Atlantic Grove, believe me. It's only a few blocks."

"All right. Well, good-bye then." After giving her a searching, concerned look and promising to check on her as soon as he could, Ray put his arm around Mrs. Maple's shoulder and guided her out the door.

Eleanor, sure that they had done the sensible thing, stepped out of the lobby onto the sidewalk and opened her umbrella, which was yanked right out of her hands by the wind. She was soaked immediately by steely rain. The wind pulled at her clothes, and it seemed to be raining sideways. Leaves and branches and other debris peppered her. The sky had grown almost as dark as night, and the air seemed heavy with a yellowish cast and a peculiar metallic smell. She thought the wind would lift her right in the air. It was worse than she thought out here, and she worried that Ray would not be able to get Mrs. Maple home safely.

The hose wagon for the New Bern Steam Fire Engine Company thundered down the street, its horse at a gallop. "Take cover!" shouted a fireman.

Eleanor ran half a block and stopped to hold onto a lamppost. A huge tree branch came soaring out of nowhere and grazed her, scratching her face and arms. A horse and a goat ran down the street. She watched a fence gate thirty feet away flap back and forth and then wrench itself free and skid down the sidewalk, flipping over and over.

Suddenly someone's hand closed around her elbow.

Lost in the Storm

She turned and saw Nick, water streaming down his forehead. "You're not safe here!" he said. "Come on!"

She did not stop to think but went with him. He led her down several narrow alleys, out onto Craven Street, and tried to wave down a hose wagon. None would stop.

Nick cupped his hands over her ear and shouted, "Inside the firehouse!"

They ran inside the brick building. A dozen people were already huddled beneath the stairwell. Two wet children sat on their mother's lap, crying. All of the hose wagons were gone. The spare horses out back neighed and kicked the walls of their stalls.

Nick and Eleanor wedged themselves in with the strangers and listened to the storm howl outside. Eleanor became aware of Nick's arm and leg, next to her own.

"Are you all right?" He pulled his damp handkerchief from his vest pocket and started to wipe her wet hair back from her face but thought twice of it and handed the handkerchief to Eleanor.

"Now I have your handkerchief again!" The idea delighted her. She wiped her face.

"Please," he said, laughing now. "Keep it. I believe you are meant to have it."

She smoothed the handkerchief and pointed to his initials in the corner. "You have no idea how many hours I spent trying to decide what 'NVG' stood for."

"I like being named after a famous adventurer. A fellow can't be named Niccolo Vespucci Garibaldi and have an ordinary life, now, can he?"

Eleanor cocked her head and regarded him. "And what do you plan to do that's out of the ordinary?"

Nick shrugged. "Well, I don't know exactly. Just that I want to improve myself, move up in the world." That sounded so much like what Aunt Velma had said about marrying Uncle Owen. She had moved up in the world.

Suddenly the wind died. A fireman spoke up, his voice tinny in the enormous silence. "It's the eye. The storm will start up again in a few minutes."

"I want to own a successful business, have a fine home, and find a beautiful and virtuous woman to be my wife," continued Nick. He took out his wallet and showed her a photo of his family. He pointed out his mother and father, well-dressed and proud, and two handsome, dark-haired sisters. Nick was seated in the center. One sister and his mother had their hands on Nick's shoulders, as if he were a lucky talisman. "You would like my family," he said. "I go home to Richmond every year for Christmas and Independence Day. We get together around the piano and sing Italian songs for hours."

Nick's family sounded like a warm and loving one to Eleanor. She had a guilty flash of herself on the mailboat, leaving her family behind.

"Will your family be all right in the storm?" he asked.

"During hurricanes Papa always anchors his sharpie, *Annis H,* in the throughway, which is a water channel that cuts through to Pamlico Sound. People say the Indians dug it hundreds of years ago. It's as calm and safe a place as you could find for a boat during a storm. Last time a hurricane came through, Iona's house—that's my sister—was nearly flattened, and we had to walk up and down the beach for hours collecting boards and tin that had blown loose from the roof to try to rebuild it. Her husband, Jesse, replaced the middle joist under the floor with a centerboard from a sharpie, saying that now maybe their house would be seaworthy and survive the storms."

"What is a sharpie?"

"A fishing boat."

"We can only pray they are safe." He hesitated, then asked, "Why did you return my handkerchief and refuse my invitation to *Birth of a Nation?*"

Eleanor could not hold his gaze. After he had brought her to safety, spoken from his heart about his family and his dreams, how could she say that her aunt and uncle thought he wasn't good enough? But was it better for him to think that she hadn't wanted to go?

"My aunt and uncle were against it," she finally said. She gathered courage to look up and study his face.

"I guessed as much," he said. "And you—were you against it?" His eyes bored into hers.

Eleanor swallowed. "No." Nick's face broke into a wide smile.

Galloping hooves pounded on the cobblestones outside. Someone hauled the big doors open, and two dripping firemen led in a snorting, lathered horse with white, wild eyes, pulling a hose wagon. "Bring out Old Jim Buttons," shouted one. "He's rested and not afeared of storms."

The other fireman led the exhausted horse out back. The first fireman addressed those huddled under the stairwell.

"We're in need of able-bodied men. The Neuse River Bridge is out and some people are stranded."

Nick and two other men immediately stood up. "I can help," said Nick.

"You might get hurt," said Eleanor.

"No, I won't," he said.

"You're mighty confident!"

He grinned. "Yes, I am."

By this time Old Jim Buttons was hitched to the hose wagon. "This young lady lives right on Johnson Street," Nick said to one of the firemen. "Might we drop her at her house before the storm starts up again?"

The fireman looked at Eleanor, then nodded. "Let's go." Eleanor climbed onto the back of the hose wagon with Nick and the other two volunteers and sat on top of folds of thick cloth hose.

"Hold on!" shouted the fireman, and Old Jim Buttons started off at a gallop. It was still raining lightly. The streets of New Bern were littered with debris and wrapped in an eerie, gray quiet broken only by the sound of rushing water somewhere and the horse's hooves on the cobblestones.

The wagon stopped with a jerk in front of Aunt Velma's house so that Eleanor was thrown against Nick. Their faces were only inches apart. She felt herself leaning toward him, and then he took her wet head in his hands and kissed her full on the lips. She didn't have time to think or pull away, only to gasp. The wind was starting to blow again. Nick quickly ducked behind another volunteer when Aunt Velma's terrified face appeared in the doorway. Eleanor jumped down from the wagon and practically crawled up the porch steps.

"Thank the Lord!" breathed Aunt Velma as she came through the door. "You made it!"

Eleanor touched her lips, still tingling, and watched the wagon pull away.

"Eleanor, get away from the window, it's starting up again. Go under the stairs and stay there!" Uncle Owen took her by the shoulders and propelled her toward the stairs.

Eleanor realized she still had Nick's handkerchief in her hand, and she had no pocket. As Aunt Velma lifted the oval gilt-framed wedding picture of herself and Uncle Owen off the dining room wall, Eleanor turned away and shoved the handkerchief down the front of her dress. Aunt Velma slid under the stairs, knees up, hugging the picture to her chest.

"My tea tin!" Eleanor cried, running upstairs. She grabbed it from the top of the dresser just as a powerful gust of wind and rain threw an oak branch against the bedroom window and shattered it. She ducked the flying shards of glass and ran for the doorway. Something sharp grazed her cheek, but she skimmed down the stairs, the wind howling around her, and collapsed next to Aunt Velma and Uncle Owen under the stairs.

"Lord, honey, you're bleeding!" Aunt Velma exclaimed.

Eleanor wiped her cheek, and her shaking fingers were smeared with blood. Uncle Owen pulled out his handkerchief and held it against her cheek. Eleanor blushed when she thought of where Nick's handkerchief was. The damp cloth seemed to burn the skin between her breasts.

"Honey, where were you? We were so worried."

"I hid in the firehouse with some other people."

"That was smart."

Yes, it was. Nick was smart. And he wanted to move up in the world. He was also a cad. Again she touched her lips where he had kissed her.

"Owen, I told you that Weather Bureau was nothing but a bunch of ignoramuses," said Aunt Velma.

"Kindly hush up," said Uncle Owen. They sat and listened to the wind. It sounded like a locomotive about to drive right through the house, so loud it made the floors vibrate and their ears buzz. Glass crashed, and rain beat drumlike on the furniture. Uncle Owen poked his head out from under the stairs to see what had happened.

"The porch swing blew in through the window, and now it's in the parlor, Velma." He ran his hand over his damp gray hair.

"Well, if you'd tied it up the way I said you should—," Aunt Velma said, then started to cry.

"Nothing we can do now but wait and pray," said Uncle Owen.

Eleanor whispered prayers of safety for Lila, Iona,

their families, Virgie Mae, and Papa. During hurricanes everyone usually took shelter in the church, the sturdiest building in Atlantic Grove. She imagined Lila and Iona with their arms around their children and wished she could be there to help. She hoped Ray had gotten himself and Mrs. Maple home safely. And last but not least she whispered a prayer for Nick, although he himself, proud young man that he was, probably didn't think he needed it.

At some point Eleanor fell asleep, even though the thunderous noise of the hurricane whirled around them. When she awoke, still under the stairs beside Aunt Velma and Uncle Owen, the silence was so complete she could feel the seconds tick by. There was no shrieking of wind, no drumming of rain, but also no clopping of horse hooves on the road outside, no voices, no automobiles, and no birds. Just total silence, as if even the leaves on the trees were frozen in place.

She couldn't see outdoors from under the stairs, but it had to be morning because she could see a broad stripe of sunshine on the wet wooden floor in the hall, with dust floating in it as if on stage under a spotlight.

She removed the tea tin from her lap and shifted her weight. Aunt Velma groaned in her sleep. Uncle Owen was snoring with a nasal tone ending in a soft whistle.

Quietly she untangled herself from Aunt Velma's arms, and stepped over Uncle Owen's outstretched legs into the hallway. She looked into the parlor, where the porch swing lay at an angle with one end on the floor and the other on the couch. Broken shards of glass from the front window lay scattered on the couch, coffee table, and floor. A large branch from the oak tree in the front yard was thrust halfway through the window, and Eleanor could see the creamy yellow flesh of the tree where the branch had torn off. Aunt Velma's hand-hooked rug was soaked, as was her prized horsehair chesterfield. The whole room smelled like a wet horse.

Next to the front door was a standing puddle of water. The cold wetness crept through the soles of her shoes as she tiptoed through it. The door creaked as she tugged it open. The porch was strewn with glass and sticks and leaves. In spite of all the destruction, the air was completely still and seemed to be the cleanest and freshest Eleanor could remember. The sky was an impossibly brilliant blue.

But most amazing of all—the road was a river! A piece of lumber and a horse harness, a child's wagon, and what looked like part of a weather vane floated by. Swirling stick-strewn eddies licked at the porch step just below Eleanor's feet. Some of the neighbors were out on their porches and, with stunned expressions on their faces, watched the muddy water sweep past their homes. There was even a small skiff, with two people rowing, skimming right down the middle of the road!

"Someone said the Neuse River Bridge has been destroyed," said a man in the skiff as they swept by.

"Was anyone hurt?" Eleanor shouted, running the length of the porch to hear his answer.

"Don't know" floated back.

Is he all right? How will I find out? she wondered.

PART THREE

California and Beyond

A Visitor from Atlantic Grove

Virgie Mae clambered across an oyster boat, up onto the Front Street dock, and threw her arms around Eleanor. It was late January, and the wind off the river was cold and damp.

"Ellie, you bobbed your hair! Oh, I'm green with envy, you're such a fashionable young lady!" She twirled. "How do I look?"

"You look a picture." Virgie Mae did look very pretty. She was still pale, but of course that was the fashion, and she wore her braids wound around the back of her head, which showed off her long neck. Now sixteen, she was no longer skinny, and her body had developed slim curves. Eleanor was thrilled that Virgie Mae was able to come for a visit during New Bern Graded School's semester break.

A year and a half had passed since the hurricane hit New Bern, but the Neuse River Bridge was only partially rebuilt, and there were still some houses with boarded windows. As it turned out, the hurricane had hit New Bern harder than Atlantic Grove.

"Amazing how it can take so long to fix what it only

took that storm a few hours to tear up," commented Virgie Mae. She and Eleanor headed toward Johnson Street, elbow to elbow.

"Listen, people are saying it will be three or four years before New Bern is itself again," Eleanor replied.

"I brought letters from everyone and even some photographs we had made. You should see the list of things I'm to bring back. It's as long as a possum's tail. But...," Virgie Mae leaned close and whispered, "... maybe I'm just not going back!"

Eleanor opened her eyes wide. "Yes, maybe you could sew for Aunt Velma, too." Then she fell silent. Virgie Mae was not much of a seamstress. She had tried to do everything with her left hand as a little girl, and of course her mama made her switch to her right. As a result her stitching was a mess and her handwriting nearly impossible to read.

They climbed Middle Street and passed the Wootten Photography Studio. "There's an idea, you could become a photographer. Bayard Wootten is a woman," Eleanor said. "And would you believe it, she went up in the first airplane to ever land in New Bern and took photographs from the air!"

"It makes me feel sick just to think about it," said Virgie Mae. "Do they need midwives here?"

"I don't know, but we can ask Aunt Velma," Eleanor said.

Aunt Velma had gone to a ladies' luncheon and wasn't home to greet them. The two girls carried Virgie Mae's things upstairs to Eleanor's room and settled on the bed to catch up. Virgie Mae got out the letters Lila and Iona sent with her.

"Nothing from Papa?"

Virgie Mae shook her head. "Sorry."

"He still hasn't forgiven me." Eleanor sighed and watched the breeze move the curtains in the window.

"Well, you know what Lila would say. 'Don't mind him, he's a stubborn old goat.'"

Eleanor laughed but didn't really feel amused. As much as she had wanted to leave Atlantic Grove, she sometimes felt homesick for it now. She thought about the waving sea oats, the pale, water-washed sky, and the lazy swells of the sound. She thought about Papa, Iona, and Lila on Christmas mornings. Christmas when she was little had not been a big celebration; sometimes Papa gave each of the four children an orange, but sometimes they got nothing. They spent most of the day in church. Eleanor figured Atlantic Grove was so hard to get to, St. Nicholas just never found his way. She had now been gone for three Christmases. She wondered if Papa would ever forgive her for leaving, or if he would harden his heart forever the way he had done with Frank.

She opened Lila's letter and read it first.

January 19, 1917

Dear Eleanor,

I've been feeling poorly the last few weeks, although that is to be expected. Caleb hopes for another boy. I hope it is a girl.

Do not keep Virgie Mae in New Bern too long because she has promised to look in on me. She has such a calm and gentle way about her with the midwifing.

Caleb Junior has the croup. Iona's oldest had it last winter and I thought he'd like to never get rid of it. If you come across any leftover flannel, Caleb Junior could use a warm nightshirt. Send it with Virgie Mae when she comes home. By the by, Virgie Mae has something to tell you. I won't spill the beans; I will let her tell you herself.

> *Your loving sister,*
> *Lila*

Eleanor looked up at Virgie Mae. "Well? What is it you're supposed to tell me?"

Virgie Mae blushed. "Nat Taylor has written me a letter from Paris, France."

"Why on earth would he be writing you?"

"You know he volunteered to fight in the war, in the French army. Mrs. Taylor and I have gotten real close with midwifing and all, and, well, I guess he took a liking to me. He proposed that I become his wife when he comes back from the war. He promises to settle down and fish regular once he has a wife and family."

Eleanor's mouth fell open. "Marry Nat Taylor? Virgie Mae, you can't be serious!"

Virgie Mae looked away and began to pluck at a thread on Eleanor's quilt. "I know it sounds crazy, but you know, Eleanor, there aren't many men our age in Atlantic Grove, and no one else has asked me."

"I've never liked him. Remember the sand crab he put in my desk and the toad he put in yours?" Frustrated,

Eleanor got up from the bed and walked to the window, then back again.

"Those were just pranks, Eleanor. He was a boy then."

"Why must you think about getting married, anyway?"

Virgie Mae shot her an exasperated look. "Only you would ask a question like that, Eleanor Hill. Everybody gets married! What's a woman to do besides get married?"

"Go to high school. Get a job. Become an independent woman."

"You don't mean to tell me you have never met a single fellow in your life whom you wanted to spend time with?"

Eleanor stood next to the window with her back to Virgie Mae. Her heart beat hard, and she thought of Nick. "Spending time together and getting married are two different things." She turned and looked at Virgie Mae. "Miss Rosalie wrote me that independence is the best route for a young woman these days."

Virgie Mae's jaw dropped. "She has written you letters?"

"Yes, ever since she moved to Wyoming. Listen to what she says." Eleanor got her tea tin from the top of her dresser and rummaged through it. She opened a letter and smoothed it on her lap.

July 31, 1915

Dear Eleanor,

I hope you will finish your schooling and spend some time as an independent woman. Find your true path and maintain your virtue.

I beg you not to lose yourself. Any young man who truly loves and honors you will wait for you to finish high school. I know this is not common belief, and that your aunt's well-meaning desire for you is to find a suitable husband, believing that then you should live happily ever after. But remember that marriage is a solemn responsibility and a binding contract til death do you part and should never be entered into lightly.

Finish your education and taste independence. Return the young man's handkerchief.

Your teacher,
Rosalie Adams

Virgie Mae wrinkled her nose. "I don't know why you worship her so much, Eleanor. She's just an old fuddy-duddy." She rummaged through the stacks of letters tied with ribbons in Eleanor's tea tin. "You keep everyone's letters, don't you? Look, here are mine." Virgie Mae withdrew a bunch with her own handwriting on the envelopes. "I've saved yours, too. Ooh, this looks like a love letter. Who is it from?" She held up a letter wrapped in a white ribbon. The return address said "NVG." The handwriting was bold and open. "Is this the young man you wrote me about—the one Aunt Velma and Uncle Owen don't approve of?"

"Let me have that." Eleanor reached for the letter.

"Please?" Virgie Mae swung her arm away from Eleanor. "I've only gotten the one love letter from Nat Taylor, and according to you a love letter from him doesn't count."

"All right." Eleanor let her hand drop and watched her open the letter.

Virgie Mae began to read it aloud, with very dramatic expression, putting her hand over her heart and sighing deeply at appropriate places. But as she read on the melodrama left her voice.

September 12, 1915
Dear Miss Hill,

Please excuse my handwriting. I am sorry I have not been able to write you, but I broke my wrist and some ribs on the day of the storm while assisting the firemen. I did not know they were broken for several days until finally my uncle convinced me to see a doctor.

I hope you were not offended by any of my actions. I would like to see you again. You are a young woman with such virtue that I would think myself the luckiest man in the world to call a girl like you mine. I admire your every mannerism. I know your aunt and uncle do not approve, but I will be very patient. I know I do not have much now, but I am enterprising and have all intentions of making a success of my life. I do not have a car or a carriage (yet!), but we might walk down to the park on Front Street by the water and have a picnic.

I anxiously await your reply.

Yours,
Niccolo Vespucci Garibaldi

Virgie Mae closed the letter quietly and gave it back. "It is a *true* love letter, Eleanor. It's ever so much better than mine from Nat Taylor. I'm sorry I read it out loud. You have only one letter from him?"

Eleanor nodded. She replaced the letter in its envelope and carefully retied the ribbon. "I didn't write him back for a while because I was thinking about what Miss Rosalie said. Then I changed my mind and secretly wrote a reply. But I have never gotten another letter from him."

"How strange," said Virgie Mae.

"I even saw the ice wagon once and asked the driver if he knew Nick, but the man said Nick didn't work there anymore. You'd think he'd fallen in the river—he's just disappeared. And I was beginning to think of him . . . differently from the other boys I've met. I feel so foolish now. I was so free with him and kept his handkerchief." She hesitated. She did not want to tell Virgie Mae about the kiss. That was their secret, hers and Nick's.

Virgie Mae stared at her. "Eleanor Hill, you're in love."

"No, I most certainly am not."

"Yes, you are, you're in love."

"No, I'm not."

Virgie Mae wagged her finger at Eleanor. "Say what you like, Miss Independent Woman, I know the truth. I believe we need to send out a search party for the gentleman."

"You better not, Virgie Mae."

Virgie Mae pursed her lips thoughtfully and took out several letters addressed in flowing script. "Look at all the curlicues. Who are these from?"

"Remember I wrote you about Ray Hamilton? He's the doctor's son who lives right down on Front Street in one of those fancy houses. Aunt Velma can't understand why I haven't quit school for him."

"Introduce him to *me!*" Virgie Mae giggled and took out another stack of letters. She studied Frank's rushed, slanted handwriting. "How is Frank?" She gently ran her thumb over the raised print of the San Francisco return address on the envelope.

"Oh, his business is doing well, he says. He wrote that I would be pleased to hear he's given up gambling. Because of a recent illness, he says."

"What kind of illness?"

"I don't know. I wrote to ask and haven't heard back yet. And he said something else strange." Eleanor opened his latest letter and read, "'Whatever happens in the future, always know that you are my favorite little sister and I would give you the world if I could. Take care of my Model T if ever anything should happen to me.'"

"Eleanor, that does sound strange!" Virgie Mae took the letter to read it for herself. "Aren't you worried?"

"Of course. I've been checking the mail every day for his answer."

"Does he say anything about getting married?"

"Not a thing."

The next few days went by quickly. Eleanor took Virgie Mae to the picture show, an oyster roast, and on Sunday they attended the young people's church group and went for a drive with Aunt Velma and Uncle Owen. On the third day of Virgie Mae's visit, they skipped up the front steps, chattering about a party planned for the weekend, and found Aunt Velma sitting in the front parlor with the curtains drawn. A telegram, a small square of yellow, lay next to her on the brocade of the plump new davenport. Without speaking, she handed it to Eleanor.

TO: MISS ELEANOR HILL
FR: MRS MABEL BAKER

MY BOARDER FRANK HILL TAKEN ILL AND GONE TO TUBERCULOSIS HOSPITAL STOP SOMEONE IN HIS FAMILY SHOULD COME STOP WHAT TO DO WITH MODEL T STOP

⤜ Going to ⤛
California

Eleanor sat between Aunt Velma and Virgie Mae on the wooden bench under the porch awning at the Union Station Railroad Depot. Aunt Velma's white powder makeup was caked in her nose creases because they had dressed in February darkness that morning before Uncle Owen brought them to the station. She vigorously fanned herself with the three second-class sleeping tickets to San Francisco that Uncle Owen had been given by the railroad because of their family illness. Neither Lila, Iona, nor Papa had been able to make the trip, and since Virgie Mae was visiting, and begged to go, Aunt Velma and her parents had relented.

Many times Eleanor had stood on Front Street watching the train cross the Trent River on the narrow railroad bridge and listening to the steam whistle carry across the water, shrill and pure. Right now the train was seven minutes late.

"Law, where is that train?" Aunt Velma said with a sigh.

Virgie Mae squeezed Eleanor's fingers so hard they were white. "I'm so excited I can't stand it." She mercifully released Eleanor's hand to straighten her broad-brimmed bonnet. "Frank has never seen me wearing a *hat.*"

"Frank won't be seeing you for nearly a week. Do you plan to wear the hat all that time?" Eleanor was immediately sorry for the way she sounded. "But it does become you real nicely," she added.

All her life Eleanor had dreamed about a trip such as this one—across the entire United States on a train bound for California! But Frank being in the hospital changed everything. For the last week her throat had felt tight and the edges of her eyes burned every time she saw anything the least bit sad, such as a baby crying for its mama.

At last they heard the high-pitched whistle and saw the train climbing the hill. The travelers in the waiting room stood up, straightened their hats, and picked up their bags.

The train slid to a halt with earsplitting gusts of steam and squealing brakes, and the blue-suited conductor climbed down and called, "All aboo-ard!" Eleanor, Aunt Velma, and Virgie Mae, clutching their tickets and bags, climbed the steps into a train car. Aunt Velma had brought a picnic basket filled with enough corn bread, ham biscuits, canned tomatoes and peaches, and hard-boiled eggs to last the five-day trip. Today for lunch they would even have egg-salad sandwiches and sweet tea.

They found seats at the end of the car where they could face each other, and Aunt Velma graciously allowed the two girls to sit next to the window. "Well," she said for the umpteenth time, "tonight we will arrive in Charlotte, and we must change to the Crescent Limited, a sleeper train. Then it will be an all-night trip to New Orleans.

Then they'll move our car over to the Sunset Limited, but we can stay in it if we like. After that, another day to San Antonio, Texas; the next day New Mexico; and the fifth day we will travel through Los Angeles and continue north to San Francisco."

Eleanor hoped they could take the northern route on their return and stop in Wyoming to visit Miss Rosalie, but she worried about the weather. They were unsure how long their stay in San Francisco would last, so she planned to write or send her teacher a telegram when they arrived. It all depended on how sick Frank was.

The train pulled out of the station, jostling those still standing, including Aunt Velma. Eleanor barely saved the picnic basket from sliding to the floor. She kept a firm grip on Aunt Velma's ample arm until she settled, with much sighing and rustling of petticoats, into her seat. As the train built up speed, Eleanor and Virgie Mae watched the small towns and fields reel by. Colored people and white people rocked on their front porches on opposite sides of each little town. Nearly everyone they passed stopped to watch the train. Children in automobiles and carriages waved and counted the railroad cars as they streaked by.

The ride was so rough that soon their teeth felt numb. Aunt Velma fell asleep after a couple of hours, and Virgie Mae and Eleanor were briefly entertained by the way her chin bobbed up and down with the movement of the train. Then the girls watched the landscape unroll until their eyes and necks ached. Eleanor had been determined to write Lila every day but found that the ride was so bumpy her hand jumped all over the page. The train stopped several times in small depots, but Virgie Mae and Eleanor did not get off to stretch their legs for fear they would be left behind. Eleanor found it funny that she had always felt so cooped up in Atlantic Grove, and here she was on a great adventure cooped up just the same, only this time inside a train car.

She and Virgie Mae took advantage of Aunt Velma's nap to argue further about Nat Taylor. "So, how did you answer him?" Eleanor whispered. "You said no, I hope!"

"I told him thank you for asking and that I would give him my answer when I turn seventeen this spring."

"Virgie Mae! How can you even be thinking about Nat Taylor when you're daydreaming about whether Frank likes you in a hat?"

"Well, how can you talk about being an independent woman when you know you're really in love?" Virgie Mae snapped back. Her voice rose louder than she intended, and Aunt Velma's eyes struggled open.

"Shall we go to the dining car and eat our sandwiches?" she said. "My stomach is growling to beat the band."

After lunch Eleanor found herself lulled into a trance by the movement of the train and the sameness of the passing cotton fields. To her surprise, she floated back to consciousness in darkness lit with clusters of lights. The conductor walked down the aisle calling in a singsong voice, "Next stop, Charlotte."

"Wake up, girls, we are arriving in Charlotte and have only a few minutes before our connecting train departs." Aunt Velma's hand was on Eleanor's shoulder shaking her gently.

On the other track was the Crescent Limited. They found the tiny second-class sleeping berths that would be theirs for the next four days. They pulled the shade down over the small, grimy window, and then, fully clothed, without washing their faces or eating, Virgie Mae and Eleanor climbed into the upper berth, leaving Aunt Velma the lower one. Eleanor peeked out the window one last time and then fell asleep.

It was still dark when Eleanor slid from underneath Virgie Mae's draped arm and knee, climbed down from the berth, and smoothed her dress and hair. Careful not to wake the others, she peeked behind the window shade and saw in the distance an enormous white colonnaded house surrounded by cotton fields. The endless rows of cotton made an interesting shifting pattern, especially when the train lined up with the space between rows and gave her a brief tunneling view all the way to the end.

Eleanor splashed her face in the tiny basin and ran a brush through her hair. She tiptoed out of the sleeper compartment and found an open seat in the car. Watching the first rays of sun spill over passing cotton and rice and sugar plantations, she marveled at the fact that they had been traveling steadily south and west for two days now and the country still lay vast and unfolding before her.

In spite of her weariness and the constant awareness of Frank's illness, she felt a pleasant buzzing in her head and a tingling on her skin, as if she were more alive now than ever. Her eyes burned with the panorama of people, towns, and vistas the train passed.

By the time the conductor announced the New

Orleans station, Virgie Mae and Aunt Velma were awake and had joined Eleanor. Here their train car would be joined to the Sunset Limited, so they had a layover.

They made their way through the throngs of hurrying people. The terminal in New Orleans was the most elegant building Eleanor had ever seen, with massive soaring columns, a ceiling two stories high, and marble floors and walls. Eleanor did not think she had ever seen so many people in one place before, except perhaps at New Bern's bicentennial celebration. She noted the women's fashionable knee-length skirts, the small, angled hats nestled in their bobbed hair, and the dainty shoes of every conceivable color except black—which was, of course, the color of her own shoes. This station seemed like a place where Frank belonged, and she had a flash vision of him lying feverish in a narrow bed.

Not long after they reboarded the train, it set out on a trestle across an enormous body of water, so wide Eleanor was reminded of Pamlico Sound. She realized that this was the Mississippi River, and that for the first time in her life she was going west of it.

By late the following afternoon the gentle green rolling land of the east was gone and the dusty red landscape stretched away flat and dry in every direction. Tumbleweeds raced the train, and Eleanor and Virgie Mae saw many herds of cattle as buzzards circled in the blue-white sky. Prairie dogs popped their fist-sized heads out of holes in the ground, then disappeared.

"Maybe we'll see some buffalo," Eleanor said.

"The buffalo have generally all been killed by either

cowboys or Indians or both," said a mustached man in a rawhide jacket sitting in the seat across from them.

By the time they reached the station at San Antonio, they were covered with a fine layer of reddish dust. The conductor came through and laconically announced that a wheel had caught fire and everyone was to exit the train.

"Mercy!" said Aunt Velma, leaping to her feet. There was a scramble for the doors, and Virgie Mae nearly got trampled. Eleanor fell more than climbed down the stairs to the platform.

The railroad crew threw water on the burning wheel, which released billows of hissing steam, while the passengers stood in the open-air station. Aunt Velma plopped on a bench and began to fan herself.

"Look!" Eleanor poked Virgie Mae. "Cowboys!"

Four men wearing sweat-stained hats and dusty chaps were dismounting from their bony mustangs. The horses immediately buried their muzzles in the water trough beside the hitching post.

"Look at their guns," Virgie Mae whispered as the cowboys sauntered past them into the station. Each cowboy carried two revolvers and a belt full of cartridges, and two of them had black-handled daggers tucked in their boots.

"You don't think they're train robbers, do you?" Eleanor could smell them—a powerful combination of body odor and horse manure—from ten feet away.

The cowboys seemed amused by the girls' stares. "Good afternoon, ladies," said one who was swarthy and black-haired, tipping his hat. Eleanor, overcome, covered her nose with her hand, completely forgetting her manners.

"Last week we barely survived a gun battle near Tucson with a bunch of Mexicans," said another cowboy, stepping uncomfortably close to Eleanor. "Seems the least you could do is wish us a good afternoon."

"Good afternoon," said Eleanor briskly. She was about to whisper to Virgie Mae that she didn't believe a word of what the cowboy said when she saw, to her horror, that Virgie Mae had plastered the most coquettish smile she could summon on her face.

"Good afternoon, gentlemen," she drawled. "The most awful thing happened—one of our train wheels caught fire."

"I'm happy to see," said Eleanor, firmly taking Virgie Mae's elbow, "that the fire has now been put out." She shook Aunt Velma awake. "We ought to get back on board."

"Where you ladies headed?" said a third cowboy with unwashed blond hair and a grimy neckerchief that had once been red.

"San Francisco," said Virgie Mae, smiling. Eleanor glared at her.

The conductor barely had said, "All aboard!" before Eleanor strong-armed Virgie Mae up the steps ahead of her. "Law!" she exclaimed as they collapsed into their seats. "What if those filthy cowboys march into that station and buy themselves tickets to San Francisco? What on earth were you thinking, Virgie Mae?"

"I don't know what they smelled of more, an outhouse or a barn," said Aunt Velma, coughing delicately. "It had been a month since those men had washed if it had been a day. I liked to have died."

"I was just being polite," said Virgie Mae.

"That was a far sight more than just being polite in my book," said Eleanor.

As the train pulled away, the cowboys waved their hats and yelled, "Farewell, ladies!" As they shrank in size and Eleanor watched their hat brims circle through the air, she suddenly realized she was never going to see them again. She leaned out the window, letting the dust blow in her hair, and waved back. Virgie Mae, in delight, did the same.

They spent the following day crossing New Mexico. Eleanor watched the landscape with interest because she remembered Miss Rosalie telling the class how it became a new state in 1912.

There was little vegetation, and occasionally the landscape was broken by mesas—some of the larger ones had Indian pueblos built of adobe on their flat tops. Eleanor saw wandering, withered cattle whose most memorable characteristic was the angularity of their hips. The few streams were lined with rangy gray cottonwoods whose silvery leaves seemed alive with ancient spirits.

They were down to the last chunk of Aunt Velma's pound cake, and the corn bread and tomatoes were gone. The biscuits that remained were hard, and the small amount of tea was bitter. As the afternoon wore on, the sun dropped low and red, and they crossed into Arizona desert. The land was harsh and rocky. The only plants were strange leafless trees that looked like giant headless men trying to wave down the train with thick, prickly arms. The man in the rawhide jacket told them these plants were called saguaros. They saw no animals, but their fellow traveler assured them there were plenty of snakes and lizards. He said the weather in the desert could be extreme, rising to over a hundred degrees during the day and dropping to freezing temperatures at night.

"Heaven help us if this train breaks down," said Aunt Velma. "For if it does, truly we all shall die."

The conductor announced outside Tucson that the station had just reopened after being closed the week before because of gun battles between Mexicans and cowboys. Eleanor and Virgie Mae stared at each other. The cowboy had been telling the truth!

Eleanor, Virgie Mae, and Aunt Velma had been rinsing their stockings and underwear and sponging themselves off in the tiny basin in their sleeping compartment, but by the time they prepared for bed that last night, they were all in desperate need of a hot bath. "If I was ever to take up the wearing of perfume, now would be a good time," commented Aunt Velma. "I reckon I smell like one of those cowboys by now. Wouldn't Uncle Owen have a fit?"

"You know how when you smack a horse's rump dust comes out in a cloud? I reckon that's what would happen to me," said Eleanor.

"You mean if somebody smacked your rump?" said Virgie Mae with a giggle.

"Not with me as chaperone, thank you very much!" There was a creak and a thump as Aunt Velma settled into the lower berth.

"Just think," said Eleanor, climbing up to the top berth and stretching out next to Virgie Mae, "tomorrow morning when we wake up we'll be in California." She had occupied many dull hours mending fishnets, picking beans, chopping yaupon, and hanging wash by dreaming about California. Still vivid in her mind was a picture of Frank at the dinner table in his white suit, telling them how the vistas and rolling vineyards were breathtaking, how the fruits and vegetables were huge, how everyone was a millionaire in California, the land of milk and honey. And tomorrow when Eleanor opened her eyes she would be there.

She drifted to sleep with the movement of the train and dreamed that Frank was at the station to greet them, wearing that same white suit, the picture of perfect health.

The Land of Milk and Honey

Eleanor was awakened by the conductor passing in the aisle beside the sleeper compartment intoning, "Next stop, the City of Angels. Los Angeles, next stop." She bolted up, nearly bumping her head on the low ceiling. California!

She leaped to the floor and, raising the window shade, caught a glimpse of row after row of orange trees. She thought of Papa's Christmas oranges and what a luxury they seemed. More oranges grew here than anyone could eat in a lifetime. And in the near distance lay a white city nestled in foothills, spread out in the pink morning light.

By the time the train reached Union Station in Los Angeles, Eleanor had sponge-bathed and dressed and awakened Virgie Mae and Aunt Velma. The conductor informed them that there would be a two-hour layover in Los Angeles for repairs, so they got off to take a look around. They could not see the ocean from the depot, but Eleanor knew from her atlas it was not many miles away. They had crossed the entire continent, from the Atlantic Ocean to the Pacific, in five days. Eleanor wondered how the Pacific Ocean differed from the Atlantic. Were the waves really stronger, the cliffs really taller, the fish really bigger, as Frank had said?

"I have heard tell that California is the land of sin and slothfulness, and it has been the ruination of many a young person," said Aunt Velma, looking around the depot with suspicion.

Eleanor and Virgie Mae exchanged a look and hid their smiles. They bought some postcards, and while Virgie Mae wrote her family, Eleanor wrote to Lila.

A horse-drawn wagon carrying newspapers had arrived just outside the depot, and people were wrestling the latest edition from the boy's arms and gaping at the front page.

Eleanor craned her neck and was able to read the *Los Angeles Times* headline over a man's shoulder: "American Steamer Sunk by German Vessel." There was a buzz of tense and angry conversation. Another headline read "United States and Germany Near War."

"I don't care what Wilson says now—how can we stay out of the war with German U-boats attacking cargo ships and passenger ships as well as warships?" said one man.

"I disagree," said another. "Wilson has kept us out of the war this long. When I voted for him, I trusted him to keep us out of the madness over there."

The newspapers were soon sold out. Aunt Velma returned with fresh, golden oranges she had bought from a vendor. Then the conductor yelled, "Aboo-ard!" and there was general chaos as they reboarded the train.

Soon the train plunged into the dark as they traveled through the tunnel under the San Bernardino Mountains.

The conductor informed them that it was the longest tunnel in America, at almost seven thousand feet. They traversed the lush Santa Clara Valley, peppered with groves of trees that would soon bear oranges, figs, lemons, and olives. Fruit was such a luxury in Atlantic Grove that both Eleanor and Virgie Mae couldn't stop staring at the seemingly endless rows of trees.

The train tracks across the mighty Sierra Nevada Mountains zigzagged up like a ragged slip stitch in and out of snow. Eleanor looked up to see the track they would soon travel on and down to see the track they had just passed over. The downward drop was hundreds of feet. Aunt Velma closed her eyes and prayed.

The three of them argued about Frank as the train made its way up California's coast. "If he's well enough to travel, we should bring him back to your papa's house," said Virgie Mae. She cradled her new hat tenderly in her lap.

"He doesn't want to go back," said Eleanor. "This is where he belongs. As soon as he's better we'll go home and let him go on with his life."

"We will stay two weeks at the most," said Aunt Velma.

They arrived at the San Francisco station after nightfall. They'd had no dinner because Aunt Velma's food was gone, and they hoped Frank's landlady would have something for them when they arrived. Perhaps they'd get there and find Frank released from the hospital, out of danger.

"End of the line, ladies," called the conductor, passing by them in the aisle.

Virgie Mae sighed and stood up, straightening her hat.

As the train squealed to a stop, she grabbed Eleanor's arm for balance, and they looked at each other. Eleanor took a deep breath. "California, here we come."

The conductor had given them instructions on how to catch the cable car to Frank's boardinghouse, so they dragged their belongings to the stop outside the depot. They didn't have to wait long before a cable car jerked to a halt beside them.

Aunt Velma climbed aboard and showed the driver Frank's address. The cable car started off with a neck-wrenching jerk, and before they knew it they were going headfirst down one of the steepest hills Eleanor had ever seen. She pushed her feet firmly against the floor to keep from sliding to the front of the car and barely caught the handles of Virgie Mae's bag as it slid past. They reached the bottom, then felt themselves thrown directly back as the cable car climbed another hill steeper than the first.

All three of them screamed when the cable car stopped, suspended, halfway up the hill. "Grab ahold of something!" Aunt Velma cried. Someone exited the car, and it started up again, grinding its way to the summit.

From the top Eleanor could see the lights of the city all around her and, off to the north, San Francisco Bay. She gazed across the bejeweled lights of San Francisco, "city of one hundred hills," as Miss Rosalie had taught her. A cool wind cut through the cable car, and the lights of the city twinkled. She was here, she was really here, in the land of milk and honey. But her stomach was empty, her eyelids burned, and her nerves tingled with exhaustion.

Eleanor had expected Frank to live in a rather grand

neighborhood, but when the cable-car driver told them they'd reached their destination, she thought every house on the block, although fairly new, looked as if it had been thoughtlessly thrown up. In New Bern and Atlantic Grove, people tended their homes and gardens as if they planned to stay there for many years. These houses lacked that look of permanence.

"So, you made it." Frank's landlady, Mrs. Mabel Baker, wore makeup, and even Eleanor could tell that she put henna in her hair, two things Uncle Owen had always called "the ravages of sin and the devil's workshop." She wore a gingham dress that was snug about her bosom and hips in a way Virgie Mae's mother would call "unseemly." "I was going to rent his room to someone else if you didn't show up by tomorrow," she said in a flat voice.

Aunt Velma cleared her throat.

"You know, he's been in the hospital nearly a month, and I've kept his room for him and not gotten a penny of rent for it." Mrs. Baker opened the door of the row house wider and stepped back but did not actually invite them in. Aunt Velma stood with her handkerchief clasped to her breast, waiting for an invitation that was apparently never going to come, so Eleanor picked up her bag and stepped inside. Virgie Mae and Aunt Velma followed her in but stood behind her and seemed stricken to silence.

"We will certainly make sure you have been fully paid for Frank's room," Eleanor said in as firm a voice as she could manage. "Have you heard anything from the hospital?"

"I heard he was about the same a few days ago," Mrs. Baker said, leading them down the hall to the foot of the staircase. "That automobile of his has been sitting out back so long it's a wonder nobody has stolen the wheels off it. I sure hope you plan to get it off my property."

Eleanor thought of driving down the beach in the Model T with Frank beside her, laughing, with her hair whipping in the wind from the sound. She remembered the hours she had spent helping him polish it. "I assure you, Mrs. Baker," she said, "we will take care of Frank's car."

Mrs. Baker reached in her pocket and handed Eleanor a skeleton key. "Well, his room's on the third floor. Bathroom's at the end of the hall. Will you be going to the hospital tonight?"

"Yes, right away," said Eleanor, but then someone's stomach growled—she didn't know if it was Virgie Mae's or Aunt Velma's.

"It's so late, we ought to wait and go first thing tomorrow," said Aunt Velma. "Do you know a place where we can get something to eat?"

Mrs. Baker squinted at them and pursed her reddened lips. "I suppose I could heat something for you."

Eleanor realized she would have to wait until morning to see Frank. "We'd be grateful for anything," she said.

"We will pay, of course," added Aunt Velma. Virgie Mae sighed.

While they ate the eggs and strange black beans she had heated, Mrs. Baker sat at the round oak dining table with her chin in her hands. "This is certainly delicious," said Aunt Velma tentatively.

Mrs. Baker did not acknowledge the obligatory compliment. "I suppose you heard about the German U-boats."

Eleanor nodded. Reading about the U-boats that morning in the Los Angeles station seemed like part of another life. "Has President Wilson declared war?" she asked.

Mrs. Baker shook her head. "No, and I hope he doesn't. Europe is a long way from California."

"Still," said Eleanor, "so many innocent civilians are being killed. Who is going to stop it?" People in New Bern, more and more, had begun believing that the U.S. should enter the war.

As they climbed to the third floor after dinner, the unfinished stairs moaned. Virgie Mae and Aunt Velma stood behind Eleanor as she turned the skeleton key in the lock of the pine door at the top of the stairs. She pushed the door open and stepped inside.

Frank's room was both shabby and elegant at the same time. The bed was covered with a richly embroidered spread with an oriental look, and the shade on his bedside lamp had fringe. Eleanor looked inside the chifforobe in the corner of the room and saw it held many fine and expensive articles of clothing, including the white suit Frank had worn for Lila's wedding. A pearl-handled razor and hairbrush were arranged on top of the dusty oak bureau. There was even a Victrola in the corner next to the window.

As Virgie Mae picked up one of the cylinders for the Victrola, Eleanor saw a tear drop and make a jagged course across its curved surface. Seeing Virgie Mae cry released something in her, and she sat down limply on the bed.

Virgie Mae sat beside her and touched her shoulder. Eleanor stared at her own hand gripping Virgie Mae's. "It's just that we're so tired," she said, wiping her nose on her sleeve. Virgie Mae didn't answer. "We'll get cleaned up tonight and go see him tomorrow."

"Owen always says things will look brighter in the morning," said Aunt Velma. Somehow the vision of her in her corset with a towel over her arm made them both smile.

When they filled the bathtub at the end of the hall the pipes shuddered and squealed. They took turns lathering soap over their dust-coated skin and shampooing their dirty hair. Scrubbed clean, Eleanor felt better. Aunt Velma swabbed cream on her face and took Frank's bed. Virgie Mae, after braiding her wet hair, slept in the easy chair, wrapped in Frank's silk bathrobe. Eleanor spread some blankets on the floor and stretched out.

"Lord deliver us from this den of iniquity," said Aunt Velma, fluffing her pillow.

⪢ *Frank* ⪡

They were up early the next morning and barely tasted Mrs. Baker's overcooked biscuits before catching the cable car to the hospital. The sky was overcast, and a stiff breeze blew from the bay, which was the opposite of the way it blew at home and made Eleanor feel mixed up and turned around.

Of the three of them, only Aunt Velma had ever set foot inside a hospital before, when Uncle Owen's brother died of a burst appendix. Most everybody in Atlantic Grove was born at home, died at home, and avoided visits to the doctor in between. Papa had never trusted doctors and often said you should not go into a hospital because you were not likely to come out alive.

They climbed the hospital's stone steps and learned from a white-uniformed nurse at the front desk that Frank and the other tuberculosis patients stayed outside in an upstairs porch. A sharp medicinal smell wrapped around them as they walked down the tunnel-like hall.

Eleanor had always thought of herself as a brave person. She wasn't afraid of driving fast cars, of high winds on the water out in Papa's sharpie, of train travel, or of new places. But sickness was another thing entirely. It was invisible and deadly and gave her a taut hollow feeling in the pit of her stomach. She was comforted when her fingers lightly brushed Virgie Mae's.

She took deep breaths as they followed the nurse up the stairs to the second floor, and tried not to listen to Aunt Velma's nervous chatter. At last the nurse directed them outside. "We keep the patients with consumption out of doors during the day so they can benefit from the fresh air," she said.

"But it's freezing," said Eleanor.

"Never you mind," said the nurse. "The doctors know what's best."

Eleanor stopped in the porch doorway and made herself look at her brother. He lay straight and still on a cot under several blankets. His brown curls were stuck to his flushed forehead, yet he was shivering. His shallow breathing made faint rasping sounds.

Could this be Frank? When she was little he had swung her through the air, but now he didn't look as though he could even sit up. She couldn't stand to see him like this. Frank always escaped from everything—from Papa, from fishing, from Atlantic Grove. He had to escape from this, too.

She was rooted just inside the doorway, staring and beginning to sway. Aunt Velma went to find a doctor, and her chatter floated farther and farther away. As if in a dream, she saw Virgie Mae cross the porch, place her palm on Frank's forehead, and then wipe his face with a wet cloth.

She urgently motioned for Eleanor to come stand beside her. "Look who's here, Frank," she said.

Eleanor drew in her breath. Would he even know her? Virgie Mae took her hand and pulled her toward Frank, squeezing her wrist with frightening strength and looking her fiercely in the eye. The squeeze and the look said, "You must not cry," to Eleanor as clearly as if Virgie Mae had said the words themselves.

And so Eleanor did not. She bent over and kissed Frank's cheek, which was so hot her lips felt singed. "Hey, Frank," she said. "I've finally come to the land of milk and honey."

He closed his eyes and gave her a half-smile.

"You've got to get well and take me out riding in the Model T."

He barely shook his head, still smiling, and his lips formed the words, "You drive."

Eleanor felt her throat tighten, and Frank's face began to swim. Had they come too late? As she hugged him, she willed every ounce of strength she possessed to flow from her arms to him, but he coughed so hard she had to let go.

There were footsteps behind her. "Eleanor, the doctor is here and can speak to you," said Aunt Velma.

Eleanor went inside while Virgie Mae stayed on the porch with Frank. The doctor wore glasses and a mustache and looked thin and tired. As he spoke to her about draining Frank's lungs several times without success, she watched through the doorway as Virgie Mae fluffed Frank's pillow, smoothed his blankets, and laid compresses on his forehead to cool his fever. The sunshine broke through a bank of clouds and played around Virgie Mae's wound braids and the escaped hair at her temples and along her slim neck. She had forgotten all about wearing her new hat.

The doctor seemed to have nothing left to say, and now Aunt Velma was telling him what a terrible shame it was that Frank's godless ways had reaped sorrow on himself and his family. Eleanor closed her ears and went back on the porch, sitting on the edge of the cot and taking Frank's ice-cold hand in hers. Virgie Mae had propped him up with several pillows, which had eased his breathing.

"I remember Lila always said your hands looked like you never did a lick of work, and I always thought they were the prettiest I'd ever seen," Eleanor said, tracing the bluish pattern of his blood vessels. "I'll never forget you coming across the sound with your Model T on the flat-bottom skiff. What a sight."

Frank smiled and squeezed her fingers.

"Remember driving down the beach? When you said, 'Follow that chicken!'"

Frank started to laugh but was seized with a fit of coughing and choked up some blood. Eleanor was horrified, but Virgie Mae calmly cleaned it up.

The next day he seemed better. Aunt Velma did not go to the hospital because she wanted to go to Western Union to send Uncle Owen a telegram. Virgie Mae brought Frank some chicken broth she had begged from Mrs. Baker and fed it to him one tiny spoonful at a time. While Virgie Mae went to rest in an empty room, Eleanor sat next to him on the cot and showed him all the postcards she had saved in her tea tin: the White House; the man wearing the Mexican sombrero; the Model T; the pink flamingo from Florida; the New Orleans riverboat; the California orange groves; the view of the San Francisco Panama-Pacific Exposition, or the World's Fair.

"Because of you, Frank, I feel as though I've seen the world."

"It is full of wonders," he said in a whisper.

She nodded to show she understood.

"You and I are alike, Miss Priss. We want to go places, move up in the world. But be careful what you wish for. I wanted to move up, and so I am, moving up to heaven. That is, if I'm forgiven for my godless ways."

"Frank, don't talk like that." Eleanor was afraid if she let herself feel anything at all she would melt into a thousand tears. She made her face a cheerful mask.

"No, I mean it. Listen to me. Over the last few years I made a lot of money, and I could have given some to Papa and you and Lila and Iona, but I didn't. I spent it on fine clothes and gambling. I'm not proud of that." He turned his head to cough.

"Frank, Papa was never very kind to you." Eleanor put her hand on his arm.

"Well, I wasn't very kind to him, either. I left him and never looked back." He hesitated, then cleared his throat. "I have something I want you to do for me."

"All right. What?"

"I have found a boat motor for Papa. He can be one of the first fishermen in Atlantic Grove to have one. It's in my office at Hill's Motor Company behind my desk. I thought to take it to him on my next visit ... but that visit won't happen now. Will you take it to him?"

"You'll be able to take it yourself as soon as you're well, you'll see."

"It weighs twenty-five pounds, I believe. Are you strong enough?"

"Of course. But you know Papa. He's likely to throw it into the sound."

"I know. Take it to him anyway." When Frank closed his eyes, Eleanor noticed that his eyelids were translucent. He opened them again. "And I want you to have the Model T. Grover, my business partner, has offered to buy my half of the company. If there is anything left after my debts are paid, give it to Papa. I want him to be proud of me. I want him to think I did something for my family, after all."

"Frank, you *did* do something for us." Eleanor wanted to tell him that he had taught her to drive a car, and that he had given her a view of the wide and changing world. He had given her something to dream about, and what could be more important than that? But she could see that he was tired. "There will be plenty of time for all this later, Frank. You just worry about getting well right now, and then you can deliver the boat motor to Papa yourself, meet your new nieces and nephews, and we'll go have a picnic on the beach."

He smiled. "All right."

When she went back the next day, she brought pictures of Lila and Iona's children, including Iona's new baby. Frank had also seen *Birth of a Nation,* and they talked about what a spectacle it was. "Imagine, Frank, we live across the continent from each other, and yet we both saw the same moving picture."

"That is a miracle, sister. Whatever happened to the young man you wrote me about who invited you to see it, the one with the lovely eyes that Aunt Velma and Uncle Owen didn't approve of?"

Eleanor told Frank about the hurricane and how Nick had helped her find shelter in the firehouse. "I have his handkerchief, and he kissed me . . . on the lips."

"He kissed you?" Frank's eyes fluttered open.

"Yes." Eleanor had not told anyone until now.

"Are you in love with him?"

In love? Eleanor felt heat rise to her cheeks.

"Miss Priss? Are you in love with him?" Frank was out of breath and started to cough, but his eyes stayed on her face.

"I . . . I don't know. He has written me only one love letter, which I answered after some thought. But he never wrote again, and it's been a year and a half since then. So his love must not have lasted very long." She arranged the blankets more snugly around Frank's chest. "It's just as well. Miss Rosalie says I should be an independent woman. She says I should finish school."

"Well, she is right, you should." Frank smiled and closed his eyes. "Did Aunt Velma tell you that Mama and Papa eloped?"

Eleanor looked at him sharply. "You knew?"

"Yes. Did she tell you Mama was unhappy?"

"Yes."

"Don't listen to a word of it. Mama adored Papa.

Theirs was a love match if ever there was one. I saw the way they were together. She would never have wanted her life to be any other way. If anyone is unhappy, it's Papa, ever since she died."

What Frank said startled Eleanor so much she stood up and walked to the porch railing. For several minutes she stared at a lemon tree on the hospital grounds. Suddenly she understood everything. Why Papa was the way he was. Why Aunt Velma told her the things she told her.

"Aunt Velma and Uncle Owen mean well, Eleanor, but that doesn't mean they're *right* about your life. 'A good name is more to be valued than silver or gold,'" Frank intoned, imitating Uncle Owen's most pompous voice.

Eleanor sat down next to Frank, giggling. "A rolling stone gathers no moss."

"A stitch in time saves nine."

"All's well that ends well."

"Early to bed, early to rise, makes a man healthy, wealthy, and wise."

They both started to chuckle. Eleanor laughed until she hiccuped and tears ran down her cheeks. Frank's laughter turned into a coughing fit. Still, it was the best moment since she had been in California.

"You ought to send your fellow a postcard from San Francisco," Frank said when he had at last stopped coughing and Eleanor had given him a sip of water. "A view of the bay . . . or the Ferry Building, or the World's Fair. "

"Frank, don't be silly. I want to stay right here with you."

"I mean it. Go sightseeing and get postcards and then

bring them back and I will help you write the perfect post-card to win a man's heart."

"Frank, I can't leave you."

"Yes, you can. I'm feeling much better. You and Virgie Mae go together. I will let Aunt Velma lecture me about the trials and tribulations I have brought upon my family."

So the next day Eleanor and Virgie Mae left Aunt Velma reading the Bible to Frank and rode the cable car on a tour of San Francisco. They went to City Hall, the Golden Gate Park Museum, and even out to the beach, spreading out blankets to watch the sun set over the bay. They took off their black lace-up shoes and put their bare feet in the sand.

"The sun seems turned around here," said Virgie Mae. "It should rise, not set, over the water."

"Do you think Frank is getting better?"

Virgie Mae dug a hole in the sand, then covered it back up again. "I don't know," she said hesitantly.

The next day when Eleanor returned with her post-cards, Frank could barely lift his head. "I should never have left you alone with Aunt Velma! Why did you make me go get these silly postcards?"

"Do you have them?" He opened his eyes. "Good, let's write one to your forbidden lover."

"Frank!"

"Dear . . . ?"

"Mr. Garibaldi."

"Dear Mr. Garibaldi."

Eleanor sat on the edge of Frank's cot and dipped her pen in the inkwell. She turned over the postcard showing the Golden Gate Park Museum and carefully formed the letters. She wasn't going to *send* this card. Her heart tightened even thinking of it. But she would write it, just to humor Frank.

"I am in San Francisco." She wrote what Frank dictated. "My brother Frank has taken ill, and we have come to nurse him back to health. I wish I had viewed *Birth of a Nation* with you. Frank has also seen *Birth of a Nation*, so I believe we all must be connected somehow."

Eleanor tried to interject a more objective, less personal thought. "The landscape we have seen is truly majestic, and our country takes many days to cross."

But Frank continued as if there was very little time. "I dearly hope to hear from you when I return to New Bern."

"Frank, no! Aunt Velma would call me a hussy."

"Let her. Ladies never say things like that to gentlemen, and sometimes gentlemen need to hear it. Go ahead."

"All right." Since she was never sending this postcard, she would write whatever Frank said. She ended by scrawling, "I shall return in a few weeks. Fondly, Eleanor Hill."

She thought twice about signing the card "fondly" but did it anyway. Suddenly she felt bold and careless these many miles away, as if all the social rules of New Bern, North Carolina, were temporarily canceled. What difference did anything make? She was never going to mail it. When she left that night, she touched her lips to Frank's hot forehead and said, "See you tomorrow!" She left the card lying at the foot of his cot.

When he died, Eleanor wasn't even there. Exhausted, she

had gone back to the boardinghouse to take a short nap and cried herself to sleep. He died with Virgie Mae holding his hand.

Virgie Mae said Frank told her he loved her before he died. Eleanor imagined that every time he woke from his fever he saw a swanlike angel leaning over him, fluffing his pillow, tucking in his blankets, cooling his forehead with a damp cloth. He must have realized that no woman had ever cared for him like that, and Eleanor was sure it wasn't the fever or the illness talking but that he really had grown to love Virgie Mae after all.

They agreed that Frank should be buried in California and put a notice about the funeral in the newspaper. Virgie Mae went to bed, worn out, and Aunt Velma went to see the undertaker to make funeral arrangements. Eleanor had to go to Hill's Motor Company to take care of Frank's business affairs, and she decided to drive there in the Model T. It had been sitting for so long it wouldn't start at first. Eleanor consulted the manual, added oil in several places, and finally coaxed the engine to life.

Eleanor remembered the big, fancy Hill's Motor Company sign from the photo Frank had sent. His partner, Grover, was a tough-looking man whom Frank had met while working on the Panama Canal. They spent a long day in the office looking over Frank's bills and gambling debts. Papa had taught Eleanor never to borrow anything from anyone, and she was shocked at how much her brother owed.

After checking her figures several times, Eleanor

decided to sell everything to Grover, including the Model T. She hated the thought of parting with it, but if she did there would be enough money to pay for Frank's burial plot and coffin.

"Best put this in a safe place," Grover said as he counted out three hundred and fifty dollars for the Model T and Frank's part of the business. Eleanor had never held so much money before, and her hand trembled as he counted out the bills.

Behind Frank's desk, as he had said, was a boat motor. It was cleaned and oiled, the most lovingly cared-for piece of machinery Eleanor had ever seen. She didn't believe for one minute that Papa would ever put that motor on his sharpie, because Papa never changed, but she would do as Frank asked and take it to him. Grover found a wooden crate for it, and they shook hands before she left.

The day of Frank's funeral was gray, and the sky spit a fine rain. Frank did not belong to a church, and the Methodist minister they found to do the service did not know him. Eleanor did not know any of the people who came except Mrs. Baker and Grover. There were a number of young women who wore veils and called themselves "friends" of Frank's. Eleanor wasn't as cordial to them as she might have been. She wished Lila and Iona and Papa could have been there with her.

After the service was over she stood arm in arm with Virgie Mae and watched the gravediggers cover Frank's coffin with earth. He had blazed a path that had shaped her dreams as long as she could remember. Now he was gone, and the future stretched ahead like a formless gray cloud.

The day after Frank's funeral Eleanor took the cable car, with Aunt Velma and Virgie Mae, and visited every individual and establishment where Frank owed money. Eleanor did some calculations and concluded that when she was finished with the bills, funeral expenses, and paying Mrs. Baker, she would have only about twenty dollars left to send to Papa.

Eleanor packed up Frank's clothes to take to Caleb, whom she thought they might fit. She and Virgie Mae both thought plain old Caleb would look a sight in the fancy suits. She gave Frank's silk robe to Virgie Mae, because she said she wanted it. She decided to keep the bedspread and lamp for herself.

The following morning when they left the boarding-house, Mrs. Baker folded Eleanor's money and slipped it quickly into her apron pocket, then said good-bye more warmly than she had greeted them. At the foot of Market Street, they got off the cable car at the Ferry Building, the tallest building in San Francisco. None of them took much notice of the soaring clock tower, nor were they interested in the water vistas as they rode the ferry across San Francisco Bay to Oakland.

They boarded a Union Pacific Railroad train heading toward Sacramento. Frank had written about the towering redwoods along the California coast, but Eleanor did not see them because she propped her feet on the wooden crate containing the boat motor, closed her eyes, and at last allowed the tears to run down her cheeks. She did not bother wiping them away.

Miss Rosalie's New Life

The train trip from Oakland to Wyoming was supposed to take two days, but it took five because of heavy snowfall. Finally, on the fifth day, they passed between sheer, snow-covered mountains and stopped at Fort Laramie, one of the earliest Rocky Mountain trading posts. Then the train inched through the Laramie Mountains for several hours before it reached Cheyenne. The people waiting on the platform were dressed in animal fur and buckskin jackets. Eleanor saw the white puffs of their breath in the cold air.

She craned forward to search through the crowd. She had not seen Miss Rosalie in four years. She herself had changed a great deal, and perhaps Miss Rosalie had, too. Would they recognize each other?

Virgie Mae stood and stretched, and Aunt Velma groaned. Neither one of them had wanted to stop here, and they had argued in the sleeper cabin the previous night while getting ready for bed.

"We've been through a lot already, Eleanor," Virgie Mae had said as she brushed and plaited her hair. Her eyes were still puffy from crying, and she was coming down with a cold.

"I'm plumb wore out," added Aunt Velma. "I'd like to fall asleep on this train and wake up home in New Bern."

"We could get stuck in Cheyenne for weeks because of snow," Virgie Mae pointed out.

"But I won't get another chance to see Miss Rosalie," said Eleanor. "Besides, we've already sent the telegram. I promise we will only stay two days, until the next train comes through." But she, too, felt very tired and sad.

When she stepped down from the train she still had not spotted her teacher. As she drew a deep breath, the pure, cold air of Wyoming nearly burned her lungs.

"Mercy, I feel quite short of breath," gasped Aunt Velma.

Just then Eleanor caught sight of a very different Miss Rosalie dismounting from a wagon beside the wood-frame station. She was wearing heavy lace-up boots and a long buckskin coat and skirt. Her hair, grown long again, hung in a thick braid down her back. Holding the reins was a large, kind-faced man with red hair. Who was that?

Miss Rosalie hurried to the platform, and a smile flashed on her serious face when she saw Eleanor. She strode forward and took both of Eleanor's hands in hers.

"I never thought this would ever happen—Eleanor Hill in Wyoming! Look—you're a young woman now!" She stood back to study her. "I'm sorry you're visiting under such sad circumstances. I'm so sorry about your brother."

The mention of Frank brought tears to Eleanor's eyes, and Miss Rosalie squeezed her hands and turned quickly to Virgie Mae. "And Virgie Mae. Welcome to Wyoming."

"Hello, Miss Rosalie," said Virgie Mae, and held out her hand. Suddenly she sneezed.

"Bless you," said Aunt Velma.

By the time Eleanor had introduced Aunt Velma, the red-haired man had mounted the platform and picked up their luggage.

Miss Rosalie put her arm around his waist. "And, Eleanor, it is my pleasure to introduce my husband, Daniel."

Husband? Eleanor shot Miss Rosalie a shocked look. "You never said anything about getting married!"

"That's Rosalie for you," said Daniel. "I wasn't sure she was going to say 'I do' until the moment she did, and even then I was afraid she'd take it back the next minute." He lifted their bags and the wooden crate with Papa's boat motor into the back of the wagon and shook their hands genially.

"I need to sit down," said Aunt Velma. "I can't seem to catch my breath."

Eleanor felt the same way. Miss Rosalie, of all people, married!

"The air is thin up here in the mountains, ma'am," said Daniel, helping Aunt Velma up into the wagon. "It takes some getting used to. You should be careful not to overdo."

Aunt Velma and Miss Rosalie sat up front under an Indian blanket while Daniel drove the wagon. Eleanor and Virgie Mae huddled under a buffalo robe in the back. Daniel slapped the reins and clucked, and the horses set off down the icy road, which was lined with a few blocks of storefronts. There were a few cars in Cheyenne, but most people still rode horses or drove wagons and buggies. Miss

Rosalie had written Eleanor that Cheyenne was the biggest city in Wyoming, yet it seemed smaller than New Bern. Aunt Velma made disapproving comments about the large number of saloons.

Daniel drove by the State Capitol Building, an imposing sandstone structure with a tall dome, and then, a short time later, the post office. "There is where we cast our ballots on voting day," said Miss Rosalie.

The shock of Daniel being Miss Rosalie's husband made it hard for Eleanor to concentrate on anything. "How long have women in Wyoming been allowed to vote?" she asked.

Miss Rosalie turned in her seat. "Women here have been voting on local Wyoming affairs for close to sixty years. This was the first United States territory to allow it."

"The voting box is no respectable place for a lady," said Aunt Velma. Eleanor and Miss Rosalie exchanged glances.

"Many women feel the way you do, Mrs. Winstead," said Miss Rosalie. "We were the first state to have a woman on our Supreme Court. Women are also allowed to serve on juries here. I served on one last year."

"So did you vote for President Wilson last November?" Eleanor asked.

"I certainly did," she said with a broad smile. "And it gave me a great feeling to cast my ballot."

"Hmmph," said Aunt Velma. "I've never been so cold in all my life."

Daniel pulled out two more blankets that had been folded behind his seat, and Eleanor and Virgie Mae wrapped one around their legs while Miss Rosalie leaned over to share hers with Aunt Velma.

It took close to an hour to get to Miss Rosalie and Daniel's homestead. As soon as they left the town, the road opened onto grassy plains where hundreds of cattle and sheep grazed. The Laramie Mountains shadowed them to the west. At one point a moose stopped dead in the center of the road ahead, turned his head to look at them, displaying his flared, mossy antlers, and then moved on. Later they saw a herd of elk drinking from a partially frozen stream.

As the wagon creaked and jolted along, Eleanor sneaked glances at Miss Rosalie's husband. "Daniel, how long have you lived out here?" she finally asked.

"Four and a half years. I was born in Connecticut. The Homestead Act in 1912 said anybody who could farm a piece of land out here for three years could have it. So I came and used every cent of my money to buy hayseed. Just last year I became the owner of a hundred and fifty acres of Wyoming grassland."

Daniel's willingness to leave his roots and come to a wild, faraway place reminded Eleanor of Frank. She felt a pang in her stomach, thinking of how Frank's dreams, not so different from Daniel's, were dead now.

"Of course, I couldn't get along without Rosalie," Daniel continued. "She works like a man and teaches school besides. Don't get near her if she picks up a gun, though."

"Daniel, are you going to tell this again?" Miss Rosalie whispered fiercely, but he ignored her.

"When Rosalie and I met, we struck a deal. I would

teach her how to shoot a rifle, and she would teach me how to read. I'll have you know I'm reading the newspaper now, but Rosalie still can't hit the side of a barn from twenty yards."

"The instruction was inferior!" Miss Rosalie laughed and tried to punch his arm but Daniel caught her smaller hand in his, then linked arms with her under the heavy Indian blanket.

"So Rosalie didn't tell you I proposed to her four separate times? She didn't say yes until I showed her the schoolroom I built for her."

Eleanor stared at the back of Miss Rosalie's head. Why hadn't she told her? She glanced at Virgie Mae and saw that she, too, was looking at the linked arms of the couple in the wagon seat ahead. "A penny for your thoughts." She leaned her shoulder against Virgie Mae's.

Virgie Mae hesitated. "It's beautiful here, but harsh," she said.

"Yes, it is."

"Miss Rosalie seems very happy. I don't know if it's because she's different, or if I'm different, but I like her better now." Virgie Mae pulled the blanket tighter around them.

Daniel and Miss Rosalie's ranch house was long and low, with a barn and branding pen out back. They went inside, and while Daniel built up the fire in the huge sandstone fireplace, Miss Rosalie showed the visitors their room. She told them that when she first met Daniel, he lived in a one-room sod house he had built himself. "He said he wouldn't build a real house here until he owned the land."

"Life here must be lonesomer than Atlantic Grove. It sure is a far sight colder," observed Virgie Mae.

"Well, there is some truth to that," said Miss Rosalie. "But when you're with someone you love, you're never lonesome."

There was a silence, each of them spinning through private thoughts. Eleanor thought of Mama and Papa, and what Frank had said about theirs being a true love match. And she thought about Nick.

"I know what you mean, I reckon," said Aunt Velma. "Owen always was a good bedwarmer." Eleanor looked at her in surprise. Had she married Uncle Owen for more than his horse and buggy after all?

It grew dark early, and they had elk stew for dinner. Miss Rosalie joked that there had been no recipes for elk in her Home Economics class in upstate New York, and Daniel said that was all right since elk wasn't fit to eat no matter how you cooked it. Aunt Velma would never have such bad manners as to refuse any type of food, but Eleanor noticed that she stirred the stew around quite a bit, only ate half, and looked a little green. Virgie Mae apologized for having no appetite due to her cold and went to bed. Aunt Velma made her excuses and retired also.

Eleanor helped them both get covered up with enough quilts and blankets, and then came out to the great room to find Daniel sitting in a rocking chair next to Miss Rosalie, his big hand moving slowly across a line in a book as he pronounced the words one syllable at a time, just as Nat Taylor used to. Eleanor saw from the cover that the book was *White Fang* by Jack London. In the halting way of a new reader, Daniel read about a brave dog, at home in the wild but dizzy with fear when he landed in the city of San Francisco. Miss Rosalie corrected only one word, "manifestation," and then touched Daniel's hand and said, "Excellent."

Daniel took a deep breath, looked up at Eleanor, and smiled. "I'll leave you two alone awhile. Good night." He bent and kissed Miss Rosalie's upturned face so gently that Eleanor's heart squeezed. She thought involuntarily of the way Nick had kissed her.

"We have some time to ourselves," Miss Rosalie said with a smile after Daniel had stirred up the fire and left the room. She was wrapped in a fur robe and began combing out her hair. Eleanor sat in Daniel's empty rocking chair and wrapped herself similarly.

"Why didn't you write me that you were married?"

Miss Rosalie hugged the robe tighter. "Well, for one thing, Eleanor, we haven't been married that long. Only since Christmas."

"But after all the letters you wrote me, telling me to finish school and be an independent woman, not to get married, I never dared dream you yourself would!"

"Eleanor, I'm almost thirty years old. I've finished school, and I've been independent. You're only sixteen. There's a big difference. And as Daniel told you, I didn't surrender easily. It was only when he built the schoolroom for me, with his own hands, that I was sure he really wanted me for who I am."

Eleanor studied her teacher, still stunned that she had

imagined her one way and found her so different. "You've written me all these years to finish my education—but you married a man who couldn't read!"

"Daniel went to work in the mill as a boy and then left home at a young age. He's educating himself now. You never know how life is going to turn out, do you?" Miss Rosalie began to braid her hair.

"You've grown your hair long again."

"Well, long hair keeps me warmer out here."

"That day in school after you'd cut it all off, I went home and cried because I'd always dreamed of having a bun just like yours. You had us all wondering whether you were a suffragette. Virgie Mae and I thought it was something awful."

"I imagine there are quite a few people in Atlantic Grove who still think it's something awful."

Eleanor looked down at her lap, remembering how suddenly Miss Rosalie had left Atlantic Grove. "The parents asked you to leave, didn't they?"

"Yes, they did. It was very hard, leaving there, and knowing there was nothing more I could do to help you children."

"I missed you. You had come to mean so much to me."

"I am so glad we've been able to write each other. I have always believed that our friendship is the one good thing that came out of that year."

Friendship. Eleanor had never thought of Miss Rosalie as a friend, always as a teacher, someone to look up to, someone who would give her wise advice. But now, sitting next to the hearth and rocking together, they were talking in such a frank manner that she began to feel this was indeed a friendship.

"There is something I've always wondered, Miss Rosalie. Were you a suffragette then? Did you attend that debate about women's suffrage in New Bern?"

Miss Rosalie smiled. "Yes, I did. I was living with Mr. Fulcher and his wife, and I did slip out and secretly attend a few meetings on weekends, and I allowed a friend to cut my hair. I was never committed to the point of going on a hunger strike or anything like that. Those are militant measures I don't believe in. Mr. Fulcher's first cousin, who lived in New Bern, saw me coming out of the debate, and he told Mr. Fulcher, and that is one reason why I was dismissed."

"I might have thought it was Mr. Fulcher. He reads people's mail."

"Oh, Eleanor, it wasn't only that. The parents didn't like the way I was teaching the class, either. It just wasn't the right place for me. The parents here are grateful that their children have any teacher at all."

They sat in silence for a few moments after that. A log in the fire crumbled and threw sparks, then a knothole popped as it burned. Eleanor pulled her knees to her chin. If it weren't for that little voice that reminded her each hour, with a shock, *Frank is dead,* she would almost have been happy.

The next day Virgie Mae's cold was full-blown and Aunt Velma claimed pure exhaustion from traveling, and they both stayed in bed. It was Saturday and there was no school, but Miss Rosalie took Eleanor into the schoolroom she was so proud of. She said she had fifteen pupils who came from as far away as twenty miles. "Sometimes they stay with us when the weather is bad," she said. "Our closest neighbor is two miles away."

The room was bright, with several windows, and the dirt floor was swept clean. The thick *Webster's* was at the front of the room, beside the teacher's desk, just as Eleanor remembered. Fifteen wooden desks were lined in neat rows, and Miss Rosalie kept a map of the United States in the front of the room and a globe on her desk. Eleanor went up to the map and traced with her finger where she had been—across the United States, from New Bern to California and over to Wyoming. Then she looked at the tiny, tiny space between the Outer Banks and New Bern on the coast of North Carolina. Atlantic Grove wasn't even on the map.

Eleanor recognized the blue cover of *Little Women* in the bookcase and crossed the room to touch the spine. "This was the first book you ever lent me."

"Daniel gives me books as gifts, so I'm getting quite a collection." Eleanor had forgiven Miss Rosalie last night for marrying Daniel and now felt complete loyalty to him. She ran her fingers over the backs of some of the other books. *St. Elmo. Little Dorrit. A Girl of the Limberlost.* It seemed so long ago that Miss Rosalie had lent her those books, but she remembered the characters so vividly she could have read about them last week.

"Would you like to go riding?" Miss Rosalie asked suddenly. "It's not too cold today."

Eleanor only hesitated a moment. "Why not!"

Miss Rosalie lent her a pair of buckskin pants. Pants! Eleanor had never worn them in her life. She pulled them on in the bedroom quietly, so as not to wake Aunt Velma or Virgie Mae, and turned this way and that, trying to get used to the unfamiliar feeling of material between her legs.

Aunt Velma's eyes fluttered open and she gasped. "Lord have mercy on my soul, Eleanor Hill, have you been possessed by the devil?"

"No, Aunt Velma. We're going riding."

"You're going straight to Hades is where you're going, young lady, if you walk out of this room wearing men's britches."

"Miss Rosalie says they're warmer and more sensible than a skirt."

"I don't know what's happened to you, I really don't."

Eleanor hid a smile. "Go back to sleep, Aunt Velma."

Aunt Velma turned with exaggerated rustling of bed-covers and faced the wall to let Eleanor know the full measure of her disapproval.

Eleanor assumed she would ride sidesaddle the way she had seen ladies riding around New Bern, but Miss Rosalie would have none of that. "I ride like a man," she said as she came out of the barn leading a bay mare and a multicolored pony. "You should, too. It's easier to keep your balance." Then she added, "The paint is very gentle. He lets the schoolchildren ride him. You'll do fine."

Eleanor's pony followed Miss Rosalie's bay as they rode on a rocky trail beside the Laramie foothills. Miss Rosalie turned in her saddle and asked about Frank and listened for almost an hour to whatever came to Eleanor's mind about him.

Eleanor's gloved hands on the reins were cold, but her legs were warm. She watched Miss Rosalie's long dark braid ahead of her and imagined for a moment that she was being led on a pioneer expedition by an Indian guide. Her pony picked his way down the path. The rhythmic clunking sound of the horses' hooves, the swishing of their tails, and the sun on her hair rocked her into a near trance. They stopped the horses on a ridge and got off. Without speaking, they stood and drank in the cold air and the vast prairie and the sharp new mountains and the blanketing sky.

"It makes you feel that anything is possible, doesn't it?" said Miss Rosalie.

Eleanor smiled, thinking about the possibilities. She wished she could tell Frank she'd stood on a ridge in Wyoming wearing Miss Rosalie's pants.

⪼ Back to ⪻
New Bern

"Here is a list of books I feel you should read, Eleanor," Miss Rosalie said the next day as they stood on the platform waiting for the train. "If the New Bern library does not have any books by Edith Wharton or Willa Cather, you must insist that they get them."

"She will look for your first book review approximately one month from today," said Daniel with a smile as he shook Eleanor's hand. "Rosalie expects a lot of her students." Eleanor knew Daniel was including himself when he said that, and she was glad Miss Rosalie, with her strong ideas, had found him. Or, more truthfully, that he had found her.

As she hugged Miss Rosalie good-bye, Eleanor could almost feel goodwill and strength radiating from her teacher. All her strength had been used up in California, and it was a relief to get some back at last.

Daniel had shown Aunt Velma quite a bit of attention, and she colored and acted coquettish when he kissed her hand. Virgie Mae's cold was better after two days of bed rest, and she said good-bye to Miss Rosalie with more warmth than Eleanor expected.

"What are your plans, Virgie Mae?" asked Miss Rosalie after they shook hands.

Virgie Mae met Miss Rosalie's challenging eyes and to Eleanor's great surprise answered, "I hear they are training women to become nurses for the war effort, and I intend to sign up as soon as I get home."

"That's wonderful. You'll be good at it, Virgie Mae."

"You think so?" Virgie Mae cocked her head and looked at Miss Rosalie with renewed interest.

"Yes, I do."

Eleanor had watched this entire exchange with her mouth open. As soon as they had boarded the train and waved good-bye to Daniel and Miss Rosalie, and Aunt Velma was snoring with her cheek against the window, she poked Virgie Mae's arm. "When in heaven's name did you decide to become a nurse?"

"When I was taking care of Frank." Virgie Mae shrugged her thin shoulders. "It was a comfort to be able to do something to ease things for him."

Eleanor had noticed how tireless Virgie Mae had seemed at the hospital and how she knew just what Frank needed to be more comfortable. She touched Virgie Mae's hand. "Something good came out of Frank dying. You found your chosen path."

"Chosen path?" Virgie Mae looked at Eleanor with surprise. "What do you mean?"

"Well, Miss Rosalie has written me often about finding your chosen path, the life you're meant to lead. And you've found it."

Virgie Mae looked pleased. "Well, maybe so."

"I wish I could find mine," Eleanor said a little wistfully. Suddenly something occurred to her. "So I reckon you won't be saying yes to Nat Taylor?"

"Lord, no! Nurses marry doctors, silly!"

They both giggled, for the first time in many days. Aunt Velma snored as the train bumped along. Life was starting to be fun again.

Eleanor looked out the train window. They were traveling across the flattest country she had ever seen, mile after snow-covered mile spinning out. Dark on the edge of the horizon was a city.

"Next stop, Chicago. Dearborn Station, Chicago, Illinois," said the conductor as he walked down the aisle. When they reached Dearborn Station, they would change trains and catch the Southern Line through Washington, D.C., all the way home.

She had been with Aunt Velma and Virgie Mae on the train for almost three days now, but she still had that feeling of openness and freedom she had found with Miss Rosalie. She felt as though she had stepped outside the confines of the train car, of New Bern, and of Atlantic Grove, and her thinking would stay outside even if she went back.

She looked out the window once more. Chicago's skyline was nearer now, and beyond it was Lake Michigan, one of the Great Lakes she had dug in the sand in Miss Rosalie's class. Her teacher had been right—she had not forgotten the shape of the Great Lakes.

Home at last. After the sweeping spaces of the West, her

iron bed and the green desk where she studied each night seemed child-sized. Was Aunt Velma's parlor really this small and Johnson Street really this narrow?

There was much schoolwork to catch up on and a backlog of needlework to help Aunt Velma complete before spring arrived. Eleanor hoped there would be a letter from Nick, even after all this time. There wasn't, but she did receive a letter from Lila, answering one Eleanor had mailed from Wyoming.

February 27, 1917

Dear Eleanor,

I can't believe Frank is gone. I am so proud of you, taking care of things. I know how very much you loved him and how hard it must have been. He exasperated me to death, but I loved him, too. Papa is feeling bad, I believe, because they parted badly and never made up.

We were all so grateful for the money from Frank. Papa used most of it to pay back taxes on our land, but there was some left for new windows and repairs for Annis H and Lila V.

I suppose I must forgive you for letting me have a baby without Virgie Mae. She is a beautiful girl, and I have named her Annis after Mama. Iona has been looking in on me.

Papa and Caleb are going up the Neuse River pretty regular now and sometimes are gone all week. The big boats go deeper and those nets with doors just shovel the fish inside. The canneries buy from them and not from Caleb and Papa. And can you believe it, people up North have started eating shrimp of all things, and some watermen actually go out with the intention of catching them. Caleb has talked about signing on with one of the bigger boats just to get him a regular salary, especially with the new baby.

When fishing is this slow the meals are a chore. Last month we ate canned pole beans and salted mullet for a week. I suppose I should be thankful we had them. Iona takes Papa his meals four days a week when he is home and says she never gets a word of thanks.

I hate to ask this, but could you send some clothes for Caleb Junior? Also spring gowns and blankets for newborns. You might send anything you find on the mailboat. By the by, when might you ever come for a visit and meet your new niece?

> *Your devoted sister,*
> *Lila*

Eleanor had a soft bed, light to study by, a warm bath right down the hall. Her life was very easy compared to Lila's. Lila's children had no clothes, and it was clear there was not much to eat. There must be some way Eleanor could help.

A few days later she walked downtown to Middle Street and looked in the windows of businesses for Help Wanted signs. The New Bern and Ghent Street Railway Company had a handwritten sign in the window that said "Secretary Needed, Inquire Within." Eleanor stepped inside. A woman in a striped dress and matching shoes sat at the front desk behind a telephone switchboard. She wore a headset with a mouthpiece attached. When the telephone buzzed, the woman plugged a cord into a hole that lit up and then spoke into the mouthpiece.

"Good afternoon, New Bern and Ghent Street Railway Company," she said in a very official voice. She listened for a moment, then said, "Hold one moment please while I connect you." She unplugged one telephone line and plugged it into another small hole in the switchboard. Eleanor was fascinated and introduced herself when the woman was finished. "I came to inquire about the secretary position."

The woman smiled. "What kind of experience do you have, honey? They're looking for someone who knows how to operate the switchboard and also knows how to type."

Eleanor had seen typewriters in some offices in New Bern. The letters were arranged strangely, and it looked as though you needed very strong fingers to press the keys hard enough to make the thin metal arms rise up to meet the paper.

"I've never used those things, but I'm a quick study," she said.

The woman smiled again. "I'm sorry. They told me they're looking for someone with experience." The telephone buzzed again. "Excuse me, honey," she said, and plugged another cord into a hole.

Eleanor walked back out onto the sidewalk. If every employer wanted someone with experience, how was a person to get it?

She walked several blocks, looking into the windows of businesses and thinking. At Bradham's Drugstore, a clerk dispensed Pepsi-Cola for several gentlemen customers sitting at the counter and rang up the purchases on a cash register. That seemed simple enough. Yet there didn't seem to be any ladies working in the drugstore, only gentlemen, so Eleanor didn't inquire there.

At the Busy Bee Cafe, a man served sandwiches, coffee, and pie to customers. The front window had a sign advertising "Tables Reserved for Ladies." But Eleanor didn't see any signs saying they needed workers, so she kept walking.

She turned the corner onto Broad Street and passed J. A. Jones Livery Stable. Even though many of the wealthier people in town had purchased automobiles, they kept their carriages, too, and still needed livery services. The men who worked there shoveled horse manure. It was no place for Eleanor.

At the other end of the block was Guion Motor Company. Eleanor stopped to watch a wiry young man whose job seemed to be moving automobiles in and out of the garage as they were repaired. He drove a Model T out of the garage and turned his head to wave at a girl passing in a carriage. The next thing Eleanor knew he had driven the car directly into the one in front of him. There was a banging metallic sound and the crash of breaking glass as his car's headlights were smashed in.

A slim mustached man in a black vest and a white shirt with the sleeves rolled up rushed out of the office. "Louis! What in the world have you done?" He stalked over to examine the damage.

The young man scrambled out of the car. "I didn't do nothing, Mr. Guion. There must be something wrong with these here brakes."

Why, that's a lie, thought Eleanor.

"That's what you said last time," said Mr. Guion. "I hired you in the first place to do your papa a favor."

"Mr. Guion, it won't happen again, I promise."

"You're dern right, it won't. Because you don't work for me anymore." The boy scowled, started to say something, and then seemed to change his mind and slouched down the street.

Eleanor started walking again, thinking about the embarrassing scene she had just witnessed. She was two doors past the motor company when she stopped. Employers looked for experience. She had no experience typing or working a telephone switchboard or a cash register, but she had plenty of experience driving Frank's car. She could do that boy's job. She turned around.

When she arrived back at the motor company, Mr. Guion was kneeling between the two damaged automobiles sweeping up broken glass with a hand broom, muttering to himself.

Eleanor transferred her schoolbooks from one hip to the other. "Excuse me, sir."

Mr. Guion looked up, then back at the smashed headlight. "Yes?" He sounded very annoyed.

Eleanor cleared her throat. "I saw what just happened and, well, I'm looking for work after school and on weekends."

Mr. Guion, still examining the damage to the headlights of the automobile, did not look up. "Young lady, with all due respect, I need someone who knows how to drive a car."

"I know how to drive," said Eleanor.

Mr. Guion stood and squinted at her. "How would a slip of a girl like you learn to drive?"

"My brother taught me."

Mr. Guion looked at her for a long minute. The shards of glass in the dustpan glittered in the sun. Then he motioned toward a car in the garage. "Let's see you move that Model T out to the street."

Eleanor was so happy that, without thinking, she shoved her schoolbooks into Mr. Guion's arms. "With great pleasure, sir!"

She climbed in the car and arranged her skirt. The inside of this car was almost identical to Frank's. She pushed up the spark, opened the throttle, pulled back on the brake, and cranked three times, just as Frank taught her. When the engine caught, she nearly clapped her hands with relief but thought that wouldn't look professional, so she just smiled broadly at Mr. Guion and pressed the reverse pedal. Then she carefully maneuvered the car out of the garage, shifted into low gear, and steered through the parking lot out onto the street. After she parked and cut the engine, Mr. Guion gave her back her books.

"Well?" she said.

"I've never hired a young lady before," he said, scratching his head. "But the truth is, we may soon be at war, and I'm afraid there won't be an able-bodied man in all of New Bern."

"You see that I can do the job," Eleanor said.

"Yes, indeed, I can see that," he said. "I never thought

I'd see a girl who could crank an automobile." Mr. Guion hesitated a moment longer. "How does ten dollars a week sound?" he said finally.

It sounded like a fortune.

"Working at the motor company?" Aunt Velma exclaimed. They were standing at the counter shelling peas for dinner. "Eleanor Hill, you must need your head examined! Why, there's grease and oil and dirt and chewing tobacco and no telling what kind of language you're going to hear. And what about your sewing?"

"Aunt Velma, the pay is ten dollars a week," Eleanor said, using the edge of her knife to scrape a line of peas from the shell into the metal colander. "I'll catch up on the sewing after dinner."

"Ten dollars a week!" said Aunt Velma, pursing her lips. "We've got to do a pile of stitching to make ten dollars. Gertrude's teaching job pays only five."

Eleanor smiled. Soon she could buy everything that Iona and Lila needed. Somehow it felt especially good to be earning more money than Uncle Owen's niece. She was determined to make a success of this job. She would write Miss Rosalie right after dinner. She wished she could tell Frank. He would be pleased. She admitted to herself that there was one more person she wanted to tell—but she hadn't seen him for over a year.

~ *Going Home* ~

Eleanor climbed down from the dock and across the slippery, rocking decks of two oyster boats to board the mailboat. She carried an armful of packages purchased with her first wages. It would be just her luck, after searching church basements in New Bern for children's dungarees, shirts, shoes, socks, and coats, that she would drop them either into the water or the fish slime on the dock.

"I've got one more thing," she said to Crabby, and climbed back onto the dock to get the crate with the boat motor for Papa. Crabby stepped astern to help her.

"Whatever is in there weighs a ton and is more'n likely to sink my boat," he remarked, but he heaved the crate on board, then backed away from the dock.

Eleanor sat on the crate and tied a scarf around her hair. It was a splurge at twenty-five cents, but she had bought it anyway. The breeze across the sun-dappled water felt warm and soft on her cheeks and arms. It was April, the last month for catching oysters, and soon the fishermen would be hauling in mullet and shrimp. New Bern looked like a town out of fairyland. The white-columned brick houses on Front Street gleamed, and dogwoods bloomed in the manicured yards.

"When's your next run?" she shouted to Crabby over the wind and the motor.

"First of the week," he said, heading downriver.

"I'll be coming back with you then."

"Suit yourself."

The mailboat passed the gently sloping bank of Ray Hamilton's front yard. Eleanor could see the wicker chair on the porch where she had sipped punch with Ray at his graduation party. She had seen him once since she had started her job at Guion Motor Company. He brought in a brand-new ivory Packard for a tune-up. He was on Easter break and had brought along his girlfriend, whom he introduced as Miss Lurleine Sumter. She was dressed in a peach-colored suit coat and hat that cost twenty dollars if it cost a dime. She clutched Ray's arm, Eleanor thought, as if she couldn't walk without holding onto him.

"Miss Eleanor Hill!" Ray exclaimed when she came out of the office with her pen and clipboard. Ray looked fine in a blue suit. His ears still stuck out, but somehow his head had grown or his hair was cut differently, and they didn't look as bad as Eleanor remembered. His hand was still clammy when he shook hers, though. "You're not working here, are you?"

"Yes, all these men getting ready to go to war leaves more work for us girls," she said with a bright smile. "How is college?"

"Oh, dandy, just dandy," he said. He turned to Miss Sumter. "Miss Hill is quite a driver. I could tell you some stories about her driving." Eleanor smiled. Miss Lurleine Sumter did not look as if she wanted to hear any stories about Eleanor or her driving.

"Nice automobile," Eleanor said as she climbed into the Packard. "Let me drive it in and check with Mr. Guion about when it will be ready." When she returned a moment later to discuss picking up the car, Miss Sumter seemed eager to leave, but Ray lingered, as if he had something more to say. Eleanor had to tend to another customer, though, and barely had a chance to say good-bye.

Eleanor heard that Ray and Miss Sumter had made the rounds of all the best spring parties in New Bern. The only one who cared that he wasn't with Eleanor was Aunt Velma. "You let him get away. You never wrote him a single letter in Chapel Hill, and that could have been your last chance at a good catch!" she said, after reading aloud the newspaper account of what Miss Sumter had worn to the Easter parade. "I can see your old maid's curls coming in now!"

"Fiddlesticks." Aunt Velma's talk didn't worry Eleanor anymore.

Now the tall masts of the docked boats in the shipyard slid by. Eleanor remembered Nick diving from the top of one of those and smiled. Strange how much she thought of him when the truth was, if she added up the minutes they'd spent together they wouldn't total more than a few hours out of her entire lifetime. Sometimes it made her embarrassed that she still thought about him and had even been so bold as to write that postcard in San Francisco. Thank goodness she had never mailed it.

She wondered if Nick would seem different to her now that Frank had died. Everything before her brother's death seemed colored with such innocence that she was almost embarrassed when she thought about it. The experience had made her over into a completely different person and was draped like a dark layer of understanding over all of her life.

Shortly after her return from California, Eleanor had turned seventeen. As usual, Aunt Velma and Uncle Owen said, "Happy birthday," at the breakfast table, but it was not a family tradition to give birthday gifts. Before leaving for school, Eleanor opened her tea tin and looked again at the picture of her mother. By seventeen she had been married for three years and had two babies named Iona and Frank.

Eleanor, on the other hand, had her job, and would graduate from New Bern Graded School in two more months. If she continued to read the books Miss Rosalie recommended, why she could practically give herself a college education, never mind Ray Hamilton and Miss Lurleine Sumter from Chapel Hill. She had come to New Bern to become an independent woman, and that was indeed what she had done. She had not yet found her chosen path, as Miss Rosalie had urged, but she felt she was on her way.

As New Bern slid into the distance and the waves slapped the prow of the boat, Eleanor took a letter from the pocket of her dress. It was from Papa. Eleanor had been in New Bern almost three years, and this was Papa's first letter.

Dear daughter,

Everyone here is talking war. It has been raining for near a week now. I haven't taken the skiff out. I have been lonesome. I have planted peas and collards and sweet potatoes. The other night I made oyster stew and wished you were here to eat it with me.

When Frank left home, I believed he was lost to me. Surely he is now.

I can't think of anything else that might be interesting to you.

Your father,
John Hill

She could never finish reading it, short as it was, without the words beginning to swim. Papa had made himself lonesome because of how gruff and hateful he could be. But now she better understood why he was that way, and he was still her papa.

The hours on the water passed quickly. The gulls followed the boat, and Eleanor fed them bits of bread. At last the Atlantic Grove fish shack came into view. *Annis H* was moored in her usual spot, and Eleanor was surprised because she expected Papa to be out fishing. The sharpie was smaller and dingier than Eleanor remembered. She wondered who was mending Papa's nets for him now.

As they drew closer, she let her gaze travel down the curve of the beach to Lila's house, then Papa's, right next-door, and Iona's, just across the road. She could see someone on the front porch at Lila's, and she waved.

The person stood and waved back with one arm,

cradling something in the other. Lila and her new baby, Annis! Caleb Junior toddled to the door and caught his mother's hand as she began to hurry down the steps. Lila called and waved in the direction of Iona's house, and Iona came to the doorway with a baby on her hip. Three children ran out the door behind her.

Eleanor glanced over at Papa's house. The shades were pulled and the door was shut. The mailboat bumped the dock. "Well, she'll draw less water now," Crabby said shortly as he heaved the boat motor onto the dock.

"Thank you, Crabby." Eleanor found a nickel in her change purse and gave it to him, along with her most brilliant smile. Then she gathered her bags and stepped up onto the dock.

She took a deep breath—the air was ripe with the smell of fish. The sea oats swayed close to the water, and a few yards back the yaupon bushes crouched, gnarled as an old fisherman's hands. The sand was white, the sky an impossible color of blue. She had forgotten—no, she had never really noticed—how beautiful Atlantic Grove was.

Jesse Junior, Clarence, and Callie ran to meet her.

"Aunt Eleanor, what did you bring us?"

"Oh, wouldn't you like to know?" She held the packages high above her head so the children couldn't reach. The boys were boisterous, but Callie was thin and dark with a sweet face and a soft voice.

"Oh, is there something in there for us?"

"Wait and see! I've got something for you two strong boys to carry," Eleanor said. "Take that crate and carry it to your pappy's front porch."

"What's in there?"

"Something from Uncle Frank for your pappy's boat."

"It's heavy as lead."

"Did Uncle Frank really die?"

"But what did you bring us?"

They pestered her all the way to Lila's house.

"Land sakes, boys, leave your Aunt Eleanor alone, now." Iona made as if to smack their bottoms, but they skipped out of her reach, laughing. Shifting her little blond baby, Iona wrapped one long arm around Eleanor, packages and all.

"Miss Priss, back again! You are a sight for sore eyes." Iona held her at arm's length and sure enough, the rims of her eyes turned red and tears rose up. Eleanor turned to Lila, who was mopping her eyes with the corner of the baby blanket. Both of her sisters' faces seemed thinner and more lined, and familiar with the fashions in New Bern, Eleanor noticed that their dresses looked dowdy and homemade.

"Just look at yourself, girl! A store-bought dress and scarf and law if it isn't silk stockings!" With Lila holding the baby and Eleanor holding the packages they somehow managed a hug.

"Now, listen, I brought stockings for both of you!" Eleanor began, as they climbed the steps to Lila's house.

"Oh, how lovely," Lila said in a falsetto voice. "I shall be sure to wear them on my next outing to the fish shack."

"Oh yes, I think the next time I go crabbing with Jesse Senior, my outfit will not be complete without them," added Iona.

"Now, you two just hush up." Eleanor put the packages on the table and sorted through them until she found the two pairs of stockings, neatly wrapped around squares of thin cardboard. "You can wear them to church." And in spite of all the teasing, they took them. Lila thrust Annis into Eleanor's arms and sat down to slide one stocking over her pointed toes. Iona put Virginia, her new baby, on the bed. Eleanor sat next to Virginia with Annis in her arms. "Iona, Virginia favors you, don't you think?"

"I reckon you can tell I had *something* to do with her," grumbled Iona, but Eleanor could see that she was pleased.

Eleanor smiled as her sisters smoothed the stockings over their muscled calves. She looked down into the face of the sleeping baby she was holding. She seemed to weigh no more than a five-pound bag of flour. Eleanor smoothed Annis's brown ringlets and touched her cheek with the back of her hand. So soft. And she had a mesmerizing smell.

"What about us, Aunt Eleanor?" Callie was pulling at her sleeve shyly.

"Oh, let me see." Eleanor shifted the baby to one arm and with her free hand produced oranges, Pepsi-Colas, and candy.

Callie's brown eyes widened, and her mouth dropped open. She sat on the floor and ran her fingers around the edge of the Pepsi bottle like a blind person memorizing it. Eleanor could see it was not her intention to open or drink it, only to admire it.

"Aunt Eleanor, I will never forget you brung me this for my entire life," said Clarence.

"Brought me this," corrected Eleanor.

"This is better'n Christmas," Jesse Junior agreed.

Caleb Junior, who could not talk much, was yanking the wrapper off the candy.

The children tried on the clothing Eleanor had found for them. Iona and Lila gasped when they saw the material Eleanor had brought them. "Won't we be a pair?" Lila said.

"Two girls in high style," said Iona.

The children went outside to savor their oranges section by section, and then the women lay the babies down for naps, fixed tea, and sat on the porch. Iona and Lila told Eleanor all about how Virgie Mae had come home from California and right away written a "Dear John" letter to Nat Taylor. No more than a month later, they said, she was on her way to Charleston, South Carolina, to train to be a nurse.

"I know—she wrote to tell me," Eleanor said. "I guess I gave her the travel bug."

"She might never come back to Atlantic Grove again," Lila said. "Look, she sent you a letter. It's a thick one."

"That's a treat. I wrote her just last week to say I was coming for a visit." Eleanor put the letter in her pocket. She would read it later. "How is Papa?" she said.

"Oh, he's an old goat, that's what," said Iona. "Two days ago I carried him over some perfectly good pan-fried mullet, and he no more than looked at me. I don't care whether he et it or not."

"I'm not taking another morsel over there. He can shrivel up and blow away for all I care," added Lila.

"What's it like at the house now?"

"Oh, he does for himself pretty good," Lila said. "We clean up and wash his clothes now and then."

"I reckon I better go over."

"Good luck."

"You'll need it."

Eleanor got a wool blanket she had brought for Papa and headed for the cottage next-door with the broad, welcoming front porch where her mother had once read aloud to the other wives of the fishermen. It was empty except for the boat motor Jesse Junior and Clarence had brought over and taken out of the crate. The steps creaked as she climbed them.

She knocked on the door. There was a sound of rhythmic scraping inside. "Yoo-hoo, Papa?" The scraping continued. "It's me, Eleanor." The scraping stopped.

"What?" It was Papa's voice all right, just cracked and in need of more use. She pushed the door open. A pie-shaped column of light split the dark floorboards inside. At the edge of the light was the toe of one of Papa's shoes.

She stepped inside and saw that Papa had his work-bench set up in the main room now. He had installed shelves, and they were lined with his planes, hammers, saws, and other carpentry tools. He was straddling the workbench and sanding a polished baby's cradle made of cedar. He looked up at Eleanor. His mustache was whiter now, and squint lines from years on the water circled his eyes. But when he stood and took a step toward her he seemed as imposing as ever. He wrapped his arms around her as if in slow motion, and patted her as if she might break.

"You're looking mighty fine, young lady," he said, assessing her store-bought clothes and fashionable hair style.

"Well, I have to dress nicely for my job." Eleanor drew away to show him the blanket. "Papa, I brought you something."

"The Hills do not take charity."

"This isn't charity, Papa, it's a gift from me. I bought it with my first wages. I've got a good job in New Bern."

He took the blanket, smoothed his big hand over it, and carried it to the foot of his bed by the stove. "Well, thank ye."

"I'll graduate high school in a few months, you know."

He nodded in a measured way. "That's good, Ellie. That's real good." He sat back down and ran his hand along the curved edge of the cradle. He found a rough spot and sanded with a practiced motion. Finally he paused and looked up at her. "They've told us we've got to blacken our windows by the end of the month so the enemy ships can't see our lights."

"They have?"

"If they tell us to leave, I ain't leaving."

"Let's not worry about that now, Papa. Will you come to Lila's for dinner? Caleb should be in soon, and we'll have us some oysters and maybe some flounder."

"This is my home. This is your home. I ain't leaving." Papa's eyes flashed.

"I understand, Papa. Let's not worry about it now. I've got something for you out on the porch." He followed her outside and eyed the motor.

"It's from Frank. It's a motor for your sharpie."

"Is that what it is."

"He asked me to bring it to you. He said maybe you'd be one of the first watermen in Atlantic Grove with a motor."

Papa circled the motor as if it were a shark. He ran his finger along the edge of the propellers. "Do you use gasoline to run it?"

"Yes, just like a car," she said.

"Huh. Will probably dump gasoline in the water and kill off the fish. If that don't beat all for a foolish idea."

Papa went inside, straddled his workbench, and started back to sanding the baby cradle. Eleanor followed him inside with a sigh of exasperation. Papa would never approve of Frank, even now that he was gone.

"Is the cradle for Annis?" Eleanor did not think Papa had made cradles for any of Iona or Lila's other babies.

"It's almost done. You can take it to her in a minute."

"You should give it to her yourself."

Papa sanded awhile without answering. Then he said, "When I die, I want you to have this house and this land."

"What are you talking about, Papa?"

"You're the only one not married, the only one without a husband to provide for her."

"But I don't even live here anymore, Papa. Besides, Lila and Iona have children to provide for. I have a good job. They need it more."

"This will always be your home, Ellie."

"Papa—"

Papa held up his big calloused hand. "A man should leave something to his son, but I have no son." The look on his face carried such anguish and regret over Frank that Eleanor's throat ached. "So I will leave it to you. And that's the end of it." He smoothed his big thumb over the burnished edge of the cradle. "I'll come to Lila's for dinner, and I'll bring the cradle. After dinner Caleb and I will be fiddling with that motor, so you women need to keep the younguns out of our hair. Now go pester your sisters."

"All right." Turning quickly so Papa wouldn't see her smile, Eleanor went back out on the porch. She sidestepped the boat motor and sat on the steps.

Watching the lazy swells of the sound, and letting the salt breeze caress her hair and face, she felt at peace. There was a simple goodness in the hard life here that she hadn't appreciated before now. She was proud of Atlantic Grove, and of her family, in a way she hadn't been before. And Frank had shown her that it was important to help, if she could. And she *could* help, now that she was an independent woman.

She reached in her pocket for Virgie Mae's letter.

April 10, 1917

Dearest Eleanor,

I am having the most wonderful time, I can hardly believe we soon will be overseas and in the midst of a war.

Charleston is the prettiest city I have ever seen. If I ever move back to Atlantic Grove you must promise to shoot me. The crowd here is so friendly, and we go through so much together. A few of the girls got green around the gills when we learned about treating wounds and amputations and such, but

I must have a strong stomach. None of it seems to bother me
much.

The doctors are very nice to us and all the girls say they
want to marry one. Ha! We all stay in a dormitory, and it's
such fun we hardly ever sleep.

Well, must close now and rush off to class. I've enclosed a
letter I think you will be very interested to see. I am sending
this to Lila because I know she will give it straight to you
without anyone knowing.

Your devoted friend,
Virgie Mae

A letter folded into a tight square was enclosed in
Virgie Mae's letter. Eleanor unfolded it and smoothed it
over her knees.

April 9, 1917
Dear Miss Hill,

It was with great joy that I received your postcard from
San Francisco. Your brother had written a note on it saying
he had his nurse mail it because you did not have the
courage. Bless your brother! Virgie Mae told me he passed
away. I am so sorry for your loss.

I believed until I received your postcard that you did not
care for me. Following the letter I received from you after the
hurricane, I wrote you many more letters without receiving
any reply. I had almost given up on your affections. Now
your friend Virgie Mae has told me she is sure you only
received one letter. I can only think that someone was keeping

my letters from you. Now that you have at last written back, I can hope.

Not long after the hurricane my father in Richmond became ill with angina, and my mother wrote and asked me to come home to manage the dry-goods store while she took care of him. So I left New Bern and went home for more than a year. My father has since improved slightly, and one of my sisters has moved nearby to help out so my mother can return to the store.

I have joined the Navy. I am in Charleston at Camp Bagley for training and will ship out for Europe the end of this month. It will be an honor to fight for America, the greatest country in the world, and help Italy, the country of my ancestors.

It's hard to believe we are at war. We spend much of our time playing baseball, football, and boxing. The Charlestonians have been quite concerned about our welfare, and it was at one of the free dances sponsored by the YMCA here that I happened to meet your friend, Virgie Mae Salter. In fact, she saw my name badge and made a point of introducing herself to me. She was very willing to enclose this letter. I sat down and wrote it during the dance.

I think of you often and believe that you are one of the finest examples of womanhood that I have ever had the pleasure to know. I beg your permission to write to you in care of your sister Lila while I am overseas and, upon my return, to call on you with all serious intentions. I hope you will answer this letter.

Anxiously awaiting
your reply,

Niccolo V. Garibaldi

Nick had written her. Many letters, he said. It was clear now—Aunt Velma had kept them from her. Eleanor felt a flush of anger, but after some thought decided it would not accomplish anything to confront her. She would not say a word. Aunt Velma had tried hard to be the only mother Eleanor had ever known. She had only done what she thought was right.

Eleanor read the letter again and again. She put her hand over her mouth to hide her smile and gazed out over the water. As sick as he was, Frank had sent the postcard she left at the foot of his bed.

She slid the letters back in her skirt pocket. Wiping her wet cheeks, she ran down to the beach and climbed to the top of the pile of oyster shells beside the fish shack. Her shadow on the beach was long in the slanted light of late afternoon. *Annis H* bobbed beside the dock. She shaded her eyes and looked across the water. From here she thought she could almost see to Charleston or even Europe. The setting sun behind her spilled a golden bridge on the water that looked solid enough to cross. She hoped Lila had some writing paper she could use.

⌒ *Acknowledgments* ⌒

This is a work of fiction. The characters and events in this book, while inspired by my grandmother's adolescence, are composites created from letters, stories told by relatives, and my own imagination.

I would like to thank my mother and father for a lifetime of love and for all they have taught me. I am grateful to my husband for his unconditional support, my daughters for their constant inspiration, and the friends who over the years have urged me not to give up.

I would like to thank my cousin Katherine Walls for graciously sharing her considerable knowledge about our family and their roots on the coast of North Carolina. This book would not have the flavor of truth without her, and any errors are mine, not hers.

The members of my writers' group—Maggie Allen, Jean Beatty, Ann Campanella, Ruth Ann Grissom, Nancy Lammers, Carolyn Noell, Judy Stacy, and Carol Zwingli—have listened to, read, and commented on this book with wonderful insight and offered invaluable moral support. My teachers, the late Joyce Renwick and Judy Morris of the Writers' Center in Bethesda, Maryland, gave me the encouragement to keep revising.

I am grateful to Victor Jones in the Callenburger Room at the New Bern Library, Kim Miller of the Antique Automobile Club of America, and David Bell of the Golden Gate Railroad Museum in San Francisco for finding answers to my many questions. Thanks to Joette Bredl of the Charleston County Public Library and Dianne Boersma of the Berkeley County Library for their help with questions about World War I. Thanks to my friend Cheryl Lockwood for her help with names.

Laura Tillotson's skillful and thoughtful editing greatly improved the manuscript, and she was a pleasure to work with. I count my lucky stars (as my grandmother used to say) that when I sent my manuscript out into the void, it was she who rescued it.

Finally, I would like to thank my grandmother, Eleanor Hill Verra, for saving her letters and for being who she was.

DATE DUE
